AN INFINITE CREATION

7

by

Ivy Lee

ISBN-13: 978-1978210288

ISBN-10: 1978210280

THIS NOVEL IS A WORK OF FICTION. ANY REFERENCES TO REAL PEOPLE, EVENT, ESTABLISHMENTS, OR LOCALS ARE INTENDED ONLY TO GIVE THE FICTION A SENSE OF REALITY AND AUTHENTICITY. OTHER NAMES, CHARACTERS, AND INCIDENTS OCCURRING IN THE WORK ARE EITHER THE PRODUCT OF THE AUTHOR'S IMAGINATION OR ARE USED FICTITIOUSLY, AS THOSE FICTIONALIZED EVENTS AND INCIDENTS THAT INVOLVE REAL PERSONS. ANY CHARACTER THAT HAPPENS TO SHARE THE NAME OF A PERSON WHO IS AN ACQUAINTANCE OF THE AUTHOR, PAST OR PRESENT, IS PURELY COINCIDENTAL AND IS IN NO WAY INTENDED TO BE AN ACTUAL ACCOUNT INVOLVING THAT PERSON.

COVER BY: ARMOND BANKS
EDITED BY: BRITTANY SWANSBORO

In Loving memory of

Gabriel "Doon" Bendter Jr

In Loving memory of

DeSean "Box the Beast" Perkins

The last thing you said to me is "They sleepin' on you Ivy Lee."

...... I hope this one wakes them up.

Rest in Power King

In Loving memory

Of

Tony "Turbo" Porter

.......Just typing that with your name next to it hurts....rest in power King.... Love Ms. A.I.

Dear Za-Non,

My friend through everything…..Z Milla My Killa….. I want to publicly say I love you. God has allowed you to survive not one but two successful kidney transplants….you MUST be special or He knows it's my job to irritate your soul forever OR you're the Super Hero I really believe you are….Let me find out. (Wink)

I remember when you were scared and didn't think you would find a kidney match in time and you randomly text me and said if I don't make it can you please name your next baby after me so that my name could live on?

Well Z, this was my next baby….Book number 4…. I promised you that your name would live on….Now it's around the world and I thank God that you are still here, alive, and healthy with your new kidney to see it yourself.

Your random text filled with nothing but encouragement and love have gotten me through so many days and you had no clue. Thank you….. I love you and I hope this has put a permanent smile on your face….

Love always, your first crush & friend forever and a day…..

Ivy Lee

My Star, thank you for never making life easy for me. I see now it is the reason I am strong.

My Yang, thank you for balance.

My Netta, thank you for real, genuine love.

My Kathy B, thank you for always sharing your wisdom.

My Aisha...thank you for telling me I need to learn to breathe and live in the moment....

My Charlie, thank you for teaching me HOW to live in the moment.

"The **number 7** is the seeker, the thinker, the searcher of Truth (notice the capital "T"). The 7 doesn't take anything at face value -- it is always trying to understand the underlying, hidden truths.

The 7 knows that nothing is exactly as it seems, and that reality is often hidden behind illusions." -Hans Decoz

"I wasn't always like this," Sevan said as she stared up at the mural on the ceiling, wondering why her shrink decided to have it put there instead of on the wall; perhaps for people to see as they lay on the couch just like she was at that very moment twiddling her freshly French manicured nails.

The more she stared the more relaxed she became. Steve never spoke. Instead, he decided to let her open up to him on her own. He didn't want to speak too soon and have her shut down on him again.

Sevan had been coming to him for a few weeks now and every time she tried to tell him something she would start right before the time ran out and then she would just stop; even if she were in midsentence. If the timer rang she shut her mouth immediately as if she were programmed to. At first, he thought that she was wasting his time, but because he admired her beauty so much he decided to let her continue to come anyway.

He shifted in his seat as he felt himself becoming erect as he stared at her full lips. Sevan had a beauty he had never come across before; simple but unique.

Her skin was a smooth caramel; the color women tan to achieve. Her eyes were almond shaped with thick long eye lashes; it almost looked as if she wore fake eyelashes or mascara, but she never wore make-up.

She had a few small freckles around her nose and her teeth were straight and white. He assumed that it was compliments of braces during high school maybe.

She stood about 5'5" and her body was curvy. She seemed to always be in place without a hair on her head out of place even though she rocked a jet black curly afro that stopped on her shoulders.

Pieces of curls fell just right on her forehead. He knew by the way she carried herself that she had OCD. That was the only thing that he was able to write about her in his notes for the last few weeks.

Today was different than her last few visits. When she first came to him she was always dressed as business casual; today she was relaxed with a Victoria Secret Pink jogging suit on and next to the couch lay her matching bag; sort of like a beach bag. He was curious to know where she was going today.

Steve glanced down at his watch and noticed that he only had about 45 more minutes with her and wanted to get further this time than he had gotten before so he decided to speak.

"You weren't always like what, Seven?" he asked softly.

She quickly turned her head toward them and they locked eyes. "Sevan. My name is Suh-Vaughn," she snapped.

Steve never blinked or disconnected from the eye contact they had. "My apologies. I always assumed that it was Seven from the paper work."

She shook her head and sat up as she put both feet on the floor and reached for her bag.

Steve put his right hand up and moved his body toward her. "Please, don't go. I want to help you."

Sevan paused and stared him in his eyes. "So, you think

I need help?"

Steve was confused and didn't respond. He didn't want to say the wrong thing to her.

Sevan gave a small giggle. "If you don't even know my name how can you even know if it's me that needs help?"

"Sevan, I apologize. I should have asked you how it was pronounced."

Sevan waited to read his sincerity and let the handle of her bag go. Silence fell on the room and Steve wanted to look at the time again, but didn't want to scare her off again so he waited before he spoke.

"You weren't always like what, Sevan?" he asked mannerly.

Sevan sat her back against the couch. "I wasn't always like this," she said, as she took her hands and waved them around her. "Needing a fuckin' shrink! I'm not crazy!"

Steve was starting to see that she did need help. Underneath all that beauty and perfectly put together well-dressed body something wasn't right, and it made his semi erection disappear.

"No. I don't think you're crazy. Just because you came here doesn't make you crazy. We all need someone to talk to sometimes," he tried to assure her.

She laughed with a sly smirk as she stared him in the

eyes. "Hmmm. And who do you talk to?"

Steve wasn't thrown off by her question because she wasn't the first patient that has asked him that and he was sure she wouldn't be the last.

"I have a shrink, too," he lied.

"Bull shit." Sevan read right through his lie. "If I can't trust you to tell me the truth how can I trust you with what I want to share with you?"

Steve sat back in his seat wondering what her motive was right now. He felt as if she was taunting him almost on the edge of bullying him and he didn't like it.

"Sevan, you can trust me," he tried to assure her.

Silence. They continued to stare into each other's eyes without either one blinking or speaking first.

"Sure, I can," she said finally. "Steve, you have trusting eyes. Reminds me of my father."

Steve gave a slight smile. He was always a sucker for compliments, but tried not to let it show.

"Your father, huh?"

She nodded, still smiling slightly, as she gazed into his eyes. "Yes, my father. He's also tall, just like you. His hair is brown, just like yours. He has wide shoulders, just like you. His eyes are deep brown, just like you." She paused as she titled her head to the right, still staring at him.

"What?" he asked as his curiosity got the best of him.

"You have any daughters?" she asked.

"Yes. Just one."

Her face frowned. "How old?"

"She's 16 now."

"Ever touch her?"

Steve frowned. "What?"

"You heard me. You ever touch her?" she asked again not backing down from him.

"No. Hell no." he responded feeling disgusted by her questions and then it dawned on him maybe that's why she was there, so he changed his facial expression and tone quickly.

"Hmmm. Yeah you never touched her. I can tell you're telling the truth," she said as she sat up and rested her elbows on her knees.

"You're one of the good guys huh, Steve?" she asked with a sly grin.

The more she talked the less attractive she became to him.

"Sevan, is there something you want to share with me?" he asked hoping to get more out of her.

"Sure, Steve. Let's talk," she said as she sat back on the

couch and stretched her arms across the back of it.

"Tell me about your father. What's he like?" he asked as he clicked his pen to prepare himself to write.

"He's wonderful," she began.

"Go on," he said as he wrote down her first adjective of him.

"Everything about him is wonderful. His eyes. His smile. His charm. His intelligence. His walk. Everyone admires him." She said as she gazed up into the ceiling.

"Is he successful?" Steve asked as he continued to write the things she was telling him. He would glance up at her as he would write, but didn't give her the full eye contact she once had.

"Very. Everyone loves him. He owns his own company and about five houses. The community loves him. He is just perfect," she said still smiling as she spoke on how much she admires her father.

Steve paused on writing and looked back into her eyes. "So, he does everything perfect?" he asked.

"Yes. Everything about Jonathan is perfect."

Steve jotted the word perfect and underlined it as Sevan threw in something that caught him off guard.

"Including his love making."

His eyes met hers immediately and he finally knew why

she had come to see him. Before he could speak the timer went off.

"Well, that's our time!" she said jumping up grabbing her bag at the same time.

She knew her time was up before she said that to him and that was her plan. She wanted to leave him feeling stuck in a mind blown trance. She wanted him to review the little bit of notes he had and attempt to diagnose her with the little information she shared.

"I can start the timer again if you like." He desperately wanted to hear more.

"Don't you have another patient?" she reminded him.

Steve jumped up to stand face to face with her remembering he did lie to her and tell her that in hopes she would open up to him knowing their time was limited.

"Can I go speak with my secretary for a minute? I don't want us to end and we finally have some progress.

Sevan could hear the desperateness in his voice and she loved it. She shrugged and sat back down. "Okay."

Steve ran out of the room and went to the bathroom outside of the main office and closed the door behind him and stared into the mirror. *She was molested?*

He glanced down at his watch and thought the five minutes he was in there was enough time to have her believe he was consulting with his secretary and went back to restart the session.

"Good news," he said closing the door behind him. "You'll be my last today so no need to rush. Just us until you're ready to stop talking."

Sevan smirked. She loved how everywhere she went she could manipulate people to do what she wanted. She always would give them just enough to make them crave more of her.

"Okay."

"Where were we?" he asked grabbing his pen and legal pad.

Steve was ready to diagnose her almost immediately because she was typical to him; pretty black girl with OCD that was touched inappropriately by her father. Steve had many patients like her so he was already preparing in his mind what he wanted to say to her.

"I was telling you how wonderful my father is," she said as she lay back down on the couch and looked toward the ceiling.

Sevan knew he didn't have any more patients today and he had lied to her because when she made her appointment she asked his secretary to make her the last appointment of the day.

"Yes. You said something else and I wasn't sure if I heard you correctly."

She giggled. "You heard me just fine. I told you he makes love wonderfully, too."

"How would you know that, Sevan? Is that something that your mother shared with you?" he asked, forcing her to say it.

She turned her head to face him. "No. My mother hates making love to him. That is why he has taught me to please him for years."

She waited for him to respond, but he stayed silent. She turned her head to the ceiling again and closed her eyes as she pictured her father touching her.

"Has something ever been so wrong, but felt so good?" she moaned as she gently touched her breast.

Usually Steve would be turned on by a woman with such sex appeal, but she was someone he felt bad for at the moment.

She paused as she opened her eyes with her left hand still holding her breast and looked back toward Steve.

"Have you?" she asked again.

"Nothing like that, no," he said trying to choose his words carefully.

"Don't judge, Steve. We all sin. Just in different ways."

"I'm not judging, Sevan, but some things just aren't

right," he said not backing down from his personal morals.

"You're right, Steve," she agreed.

"Can we start from the beginning?" he asked.

"The beginning to what?" she asked, to be clear.

"Let's just go back as far as you can remember. As a kid perhaps? And then go until we get to where we are now?"

She nodded still staring at the ceiling as the sexy feeling she had a few minutes ago faded and she was forced to remember things she attempted bury forever. She placed both of her hands across her stomach one on top of the other.

"Okay, let's start from when I was a kid."

You're almost a woman!

"Hurry up, Jon! We are going to be late!" Gianni yelled to her husband as she put her diamond stud in her right ear.

Sevan lay across her parent's king-sized bed as she watched her mom dress for a black-tie event that was made to honor her father Jonathon for all that he had done in the community. Businessman of the year is what the city of Cleveland called him.

"He always does this," she mumbled to herself as she oiled her smooth cocoa legs. "Man will be late for his own funeral, I swear!

Little did she know Jonathon was already dressed and waiting for her in the family room of their 4,785-square foot home in Pepper Pike. He could hear her yelling, but he didn't care because she was the one that was always late getting ready.

"You look pretty, Mommy." Sevan said, as she admired her mother's beauty.

Sevan was a perfect mixture of her parents. She had features of her mother; almond eyes, bright smile with full lips; but because her mother was black, and her father was white; she had curly hair while her mother had thick coarse hair that she kept a relaxer in because she was always ashamed of how her hair was too "black" to her. She envied how light Sevan was and how "pretty" her hair was. She was jealous at how since

Sevan was born Jonathan gave all of his attention to Sevan. She had become his world and he paid Gianni very little attention unless they were in public and he needed the camera crews to believe they were happy and in love. No one could fathom the things that went on behind those walls.

Gianni didn't respond to Sevan she just stood up and slipped on her little black dress as she admired her figure in the full mirrors by her closet doors.

"Go tell your father I'm ready."

Sevan was used to being ignored by her mother and did just as she was told as she cut her eyes at her. Gianni caught the stare and turned her attention toward Sevan.

"I saw that! Look at me like that again and you won't see your 13th birthday!" she snapped as she pointed at her.

Sevan changed her facial expression. "Yes, ma'am," she said, as she hurried out the room and down the stairs toward the family room.

He father was sitting on the couch staring out the window as if he were in deep thought. He was a very handsome man that women flocked to, but he never gave them the time of day. He was known as the most faithful man ever and so many women would say how Gianni was so lucky to have such a wonderful family man who only had eyes for her.

"Daddy?" Sevan said, as she walked toward him slowly.

He turned his head to her and smiled. His face always lit up when he saw her. Sevan loved her father very much and often wondered why the love felt wrong to her. There wasn't anything he wouldn't do for her.

"Hey, Baby Girl," he said as he reached his hands out to her to come closer.

She hesitantly walked over to him glancing behind her. "Hey."

He pulled her on the couch next to him as he put his left arm around her. She laid her head on his shoulder and closed her eyes as she inhaled the scent of his *Gucci Guilty Black* cologne. He always smelled so good. He kissed her forehead and pulled her closer to him.

"Mommy said she's ready," she said with her eyes closed still enjoying the affection he was giving her right now.

"Finally. What about you though? Are you ready?" he asked.

She opened her eyes and sat straight up. "For?"

He smiled. "Your 13th birthday. You'll almost be a woman when I get back home tonight!" he chuckled.

She smiled a semi smile. "I guess so."

"Guess so? What do you want for your birthday?" he asked, as he placed his right hand on her right thigh.

Sevan felt a slight discomfort. She always felt like this whenever he touched her. This wasn't the first time he touched her, and she knew it wouldn't be the last. Every time he would touch her like this she would feel a sense of unease then he would do something to relax her. She could feel the dysfunctional love he was giving her was becoming functional to her, but he was her father, so he wouldn't intentionally hurt her, right?

"I don't want anything, Daddy," she humbly said.

He smiled. His smile was so inviting yet so deceiving. He looked back toward the door and Gianni was standing there staring at him with eyes filled with daggers. She hated their relationship and wished he still looked at her like that.

"I'm ready." She snapped.

"Okay, I'll meet you in the car," he said as he gave her an evil stare until she finally walked away.

"Will you be asleep when I get home?" he asked Sevan.

She shrugged. "Probably. You know I don't care much for birthdays."

He smiled as he took his left hand and softly touched her cheek. "So humble and so beautiful. Don't change."

She smiled. "I won't, Daddy."

He glanced around again before he reached in and kissed her lips softly. This wasn't their first kiss, so she knew it was coming when he touched her cheek. She used to cringe, but the smell of his cologne and soft touches relaxed her this time so she closed her eyes and returned the kiss.

XXX

She could feel something happening inside of her body and her stomach as she took in his cologne and his soft touches. She hated it and she loved it at the same time and it was driving her insane and she didn't know who to tell or if she should because her father is someone that she's supposed to trust, right?

He pulled back and stood up in front of her and she could see his erection through his black tuxedo. He smiled as he saw her eyes go straight to it and back to him. He reached down and grabbed her right hand and put it on it.

"See what you do to me?" he whispered.

She didn't respond. She just looked him in his eyes waiting to see what he was going to say next. She had never slept with her father and they never did more than kiss. Sometimes he would rub her thighs and massage her back, but never touched her in other places. His touches were always gentle, but she knew deep down it was inappropriate. One time he came in the bathroom and watched her shower as he touched himself, but he never physically touched her.

Sevan didn't respond she just stared into his eyes as he gazed back at her. His look was different than normal, and she couldn't put a finger on what he was thinking.

"See you in a few hours," he said as he adjusted his pants and walked out of the room.

Sevan sat there alone staring out the window as she watched the black Bentley pull out of the driveway. She could see her mother's shadow of her waving her arms around and she knew they were having their regular argument before they went to an event.

Sevan shifted in her seat as she felt her panties feel like she had peed on herself and became embarrassed and quickly ran to the bathroom to check herself. When she sat on the toilet there was nothing but clear fluids coming out of her and she didn't know what it was. She wiped herself down and jumped into the shower to clean herself off then go to bed.

As she slept in her queen-sized bed she felt relaxed and felt herself dreaming until she heard a loud thump as her bedroom door flew open and scared her out of her sleep. She jumped up to see her mother drunk standing over her. Her up do she had of curls was hanging down over her head and her mascara was running down her face as if she had been crying for hours and her lipstick was smudged. She had on one heel still and the other was in her right hand. She pointed the heel towards Sevan's face as she sat up backing up against the headboard in fear wondering what she had done.

She thought about her chores and remembered she finished everything that was left for her to do so she was clueless and in complete fear of her right now and wondered where her father was.

"YOU!" her mother yelled still pointing the heel toward her as she stumbled to keep her balance.

"What did I do?" Sevan asked out of fear.

"You! I should have never had you! You want my man

and you been workin' your hand to get him!" she yelled through tears.

Sevan had no idea what she was talking about. She didn't want her father, she didn't want the attention he gave her that he should have been giving her mother.

"No, Mommy. No, I don't." she said softly as tears began to fall.

"Oh, now you wanna cry now that I called you on your shit! Were you crying when you were thinking about taking him from me?" she sneered as she eased in to her.

Just then her father walked in the room and grabbed her mother from behind, picking her up slightly to get her out of Sevan's face.

"What are you doing? Leave this girl alone!" he said dragging her out.

"Leave him alone! You can't have him! He's mine!" she screamed as Jonathan drug her down the hall to their bedroom.

Sevan was shaking as she heard their bedroom door slam then she could faintly hear them arguing and the door reopened, and she heard her father say he was sleeping in the guest room as he slammed the door behind him.

She heard her mother scream through tears, "Jonnnnnnn! Come back! Please come baaacccck!"

She could hear her mother crying for about 20 more

xxxiii

minutes, then the whole house was silent. She could see the hallway way light glare through the bedroom door and was afraid to lay back down because she wasn't sure what was next. She glanced over at the clock on her night stand and saw that it was 3:40 a.m. She wondered what set her mother off and then she wondered if her mother knew or noticed her father's behaviors toward her why would she allow him to be like that or why was she blaming her? Was it really something she was doing and that is why her father felt it was ok to be like this with her?

As she lay there trying to fall back to sleep and calm her nerves she saw her father appear in the door way.

"Are you okay?" he asked.

Sevan shook her head. "What did I do?"

Jonathan looked down the hallway before walking into her room and closing the door lightly behind him. Sevan noticed him turn the lock behind him as he closed it. Her heart raced faster than when her mother was standing over her screaming.

"You didn't do anything," he said as he sat on her bed and placed his left hand on her legs to comfort her.

She felt a sudden feeling come over her that she couldn't describe when his hand made contact to her body. Once again, she felt uneasy then a slight comfort followed.

"She can't hold her liquor. I should have just let her go to work instead of coming with me," he said as he shook his head.

Gianni was the head nurse at Cleveland General Hospital and whenever Jonathan had an event such as tonight's she was always sure to take off because she loved being in the spotlight with her husband.

"Why does she hate me so much?" Sevan had to know as she felt tears coming down her face.

Jonathan reached over and wiped them off softly. "She's just jealous of you. Jealous of you and I and how close we are. Don't worry baby, I will always protect you from her and anyone else." He assured her as he began to caress her face and slowly move his hands down her body.

His touches felt good like they always did; soft and secure feeling. She could feel herself relaxing as her heart rate began to go back to a normal pace.

"I have to make it up to you. This is no way anyone should come into their 13th birthday."

Sevan didn't say a word. She just glared at him with the little light that the moon provided through her blinds wondering what was next.

Jonathan became quiet as he slid her night gown over her head and sat it on the pillow next to her. Sevan's heart rate began to pick up again.

Her father was sitting there with his dress shirt on with the top button open as his bow tie hung around the collar. He continued to stare at her body analyzing it while he caressed her slowly as she saw his right hand unzip his pants and slide in through the zipper part.

"Take off your panties." He whispered.

Sevan didn't move. She was afraid to move, and she felt mute. She didn't know what he was going to do next. Jonathan waited for a moment and stopped caressing her and himself.

"Take off your panties." He repeated but this time with authority in his voice.

Sevan did as she was told.

"I'm not going to hurt you. I want to make it up to you," he assured her.

"Daddy- "she whispered, as another tear streamed her cheek.

"I will never hurt you," he promised her.

Jonathan stood up and gently took Sevan by the legs and turned her alongside of the bed to face him. Her legs and body began to tremble as he gently lay his body on top of hers. Another tear fell. Jonathon kissed this one this time and then wiped it off and began to kiss her lips. She didn't return the kiss this time.

"Kiss me," he instructed.

She paused and stared him in the eyes.

"Kiss me," he repeated. "You are the only one that can make me feel good."

7

She didn't know what else to do except do as he said. She began to kiss him as tears continued to pour. He started to kiss her neck slowly and she thought it felt good, but the tears wouldn't stop. He started to kiss her body gently and it felt good, but the tears continued. When he reached between her legs he took his time as he started to kiss her some more. She felt him kiss a spot that made her entire body jerk and her legs tremble. The tears poured silently because she felt deep inside it was so wrong, but whatever he was doing to her felt so good.

She felt her body tremble and her legs began to shake and she thought she had to pee as he continued to kiss her until she felt as though her body exploded. She felt so good and so dirty at the same time and she didn't know why she felt like that. When her body reached its peak, she collapsed, and he laid on the bed next to her and pulled her close to him and held her.

"I love you Sevan."

Sevan was still crying, but felt a sense of relief she had never felt before and she cuddled closer to her father. "I love you too, Daddy."

"I was just a kid!" Sevan cried to Steve.

"I am so sorry he did that to you. Did he ever penetrate you or was that the only time he touched you?" Steve asked.

xxxvii

"No. We didn't have sex until my 16th birthday when I became a "real woman"."

Steve was disgusted at her story and how someone so loved in the community was so sick mentally.

"Do you need a minute?" he asked to be make sure he met her needs.

"Yes. Can you get me some water please?"

"Sure."

A real woman

"Surprise! Happy Sweet 16!" everyone yelled as Sevan walked into the house from track practice to a crowd of people she barely knew or ever saw.

She knew this party wasn't really for her, but for her father and mother to look good in front of the community. Giving their only daughter a sweet 16 surprise party while the invitations were only extended to prestigious names and reporter friends. Anything to keep his name sake looking like the perfect family man.

Sevan was used to this, so she tried to slip into her perfect daughter mode and keep the act going for the man of her life.

"Oh, wow!" she screamed, with a fake smile to match.

Sevan's eye immediately went to her parents who were standing in front of the small crowd of people who would die to switch places with her just to be a part of Jonathan's life. She dropped her gym bag next to the front door and walked towards them as if this scene was rehearsed many times before there were an audience.

"We just wanted to make sure you had a wonderful Birthday, Sweetheart!" her mother said in a perfect TV sitcom mom's voice.

Sevan kept her head straight, but allowed her eyes to

look to her left to meet her mother's eyes as she kept the act going. This was probably the nicest her mother ever was to her since the day she stormed in her room three years ago accusing her of wanting *her* man.

Sevan and Gianni's mother/daughter relationship ended that night and turned into two women competing for the same man's love. The only problem was Gianni was competing while Sevan was praying every night to a god that she was starting to believe either hated her or didn't exist at all, that he would allow Gianni to win this war between them and her father would just leave her alone.

The older Sevan got and the more woman like her figure grew the more Gianni's hate grew for her. She wasn't the average teen that went through acne or the odd transition years, no Sevan seemed to become more and more beautiful every day.

Gianni never came at Sevan the way she did on her birthday that night again because Jonathan assured her that if she ever touched her or scared her again he would leave her and do it publicly so that he could embarrass and shame her name and his reason would be he had to take his only daughter and protect her from the abuse of a drunken mother.

Gianni knew he was telling the truth and she dared not challenge him since she had worked so hard to be in the position she was in at Cleveland General Hospital so instead she would just give her evil stares and snide remarks every chance she got. Sevan used to accept it, but as time grew on and so did she and she was slowly learning to defend herself to her mother and would return the stares or sarcastic comments.

Jonathan moved closer to Sevan with open arms to hug her. Sevan's first instinct was to move back, but she quickly caught herself so that she didn't alarm her guest as to why she would jump from such a wonderful father and she reminded herself she was in character right now and to stick to the script and she moved into his hug returning it.

Her mother smiled, but her eyes told a different story. She wondered how they had the entire room hypnotized to not catch the looks and read the true vibes they were putting out.

"Happy Birthday, Baby Girl," he said as he tightened his hug and kissed her forehead.

"Thank you, Daddy," Sevan said softly.

"I just want you to have the best Birthday ever!" he said.

Sevan froze inside when he said that. On her 14th birthday when he said that he met her in her room late that night to allow her to feel what his *magic fingers* can do to her body. On her 15th birthday he wanted to teach her how a young woman would please her man with her mouth. She could only imagine what her 16th birthday would be as he promised that he would *make love* to her. If this is what love is that he was showing her she feared what making love would be like.

At times, Sevan thought that her mother knew exactly what was going on and because she despised her so much she allowed it just to see Sevan in pain and dying slowly inside. She often wondered what she did so wrong that even God had closed his ears to her cries for help.

"It's wonderful, Daddy," she lied in her sweetest voice possible.

"Go socialize with your friends, it's a party," he instructed.

Friends? She didn't even go to school with any of the teens there, but she did as she was told. During the party from across the room she would catch her father staring at her and when one of his golfing buddie's son, Trey, who had a crush on her would come near her to talk he would give her a look like a jealous boyfriend and she knew that meant to walk away from Trey.

Trey thought she was playing hard to get, while Gianni noticed every look between them. Gianni would try and flirt softly with some of the single men there to get Jonathan's attention, but he never acknowledged her childish attempts to get a rise out of him. Inside she was furious, but on the outside she was the happiest wife in the room as other wives envied her.

Sevan had begun to relax after she snuck a few shots of Jack Daniels when no was watching and started to open up and talk and laugh more with the crowd. Her father was ecstatic at how she was impressing the people watching because it made him appear perfect. Trey was addicted to Sevan's smile and even though she would go to the other side of the room when he would come near, he didn't care he just would follow her. After the liquor kicked in she stopped running from him and began to flirt with him.

"You having fun?" Trey asked as he stared into her eyes.

Trey was handsome and taller than she was. He stood about 6'2" and kept a low hair cut with brush waves. He was brown skinned, completely opposite of her father and had a smile that lit up the room. She was attracted to him and she had never noticed him the way she was right now.

"Yeah, I am now. You?" she said giving him a seductive look with her eyes.

Jonathan knew the look she was giving as he stared at them from across the room ignoring the people that were having a conversation he mentally drifted away from. Sevan had sex appeal and she knew how to seduce a man but didn't really know that that's what she was doing.

"Yes. I really think you are beautiful," he burst out, as if he were dying to say that to her all evening.

She paused, and her smile slowly faded. She hated hearing she was beautiful since that's all her father ever said to her right before he did whatever he felt like doing to her.

"Thanks, Trey," she said dryly.

"Did I say something wrong?" he asked out of genuine concern.

"She's just shy," her father said, as he crept up and slid his right arm around her.

Sevan stopped smiling completely because she was

startled by him and didn't see him coming over, but she knew it was only a matter of time before he did.

"Trey, right?" he asked, as he extended his right hand to him.

"Yes, Sir," he mannerly responded as he shook his hand.

Jonathan gripped Trey's hand firmer than usual as Trey was confused by it and he released it and put it back around Sevan. Trey felt a weird energy between them right now and waited to see what he was going to say next.

"I haven't seen you since you were a kid." Jonathan started small talk, never releasing eye contact or his grip on Sevan.

Trey glanced toward Sevan and noticed she seemed uncomfortable. Her smile was gone, and she was sober again. She knew her father wasn't there to do a regular "protect my daughter" conversation, but moreso this is my woman get your own; sort of like a dog pissing on his territory.

Trey was older than Sevan, 18, and a senior about to graduate high school and then off to college, so he could pick up on Jonathan's strange behavior right now. He wasn't oblivious to things as other's in the room were.

"Yeah, I'm almost a grown man now." Trey said as he deepened his voice.

Jonathan laughed at him. "Yes, you are. And too grown to be around my underage daughter."

Trey knew where he was headed and decided to step back because he had his whole life ahead of him and Jonathan was well respected and so was Trey's father, so he knew how to choose his battles. He just head nodded Jonathan to let him know he understood what he was saying and decided to end the conversation so as not embarrass his own father.

"Understood, Sir." He turned his attention to Sevan. "Happy Birthday." And he walked back toward his father.

Sevan hated her father even more right now and she hated how Trey gave up so easily. If God wouldn't save her and her mother didn't care enough to save her who would?

"What was that about?" Trey's father whispered still smiling so that he didn't let his looks give him away.

"I don't know, but there's something not right about them," he said with his back facing Sevan and her father.

Trey's father didn't say anything to his response, but decided to pay closer attention to whatever his son picked up on.

Jonathan turned Sevan around with his arms still gripping her as he smiled and walked her around the party talking quietly to her.

"I don't want to see that shit again."

She didn't say a word. She was becoming numb and wanted more alcohol.

"You know how that makes you look? All in some boy's face? You look like a slut," he said, as he kept a smile on his face while they walked around.

She stayed silent and he kissed her forehead as he stopped in front of the pack of teenage girls that were huddled up talking. They all had crushes on Jonathan just as their mothers did.

"Hello, Mr. White," the teens eagerly said together while blushing.

"Hello, ladies," he said smiling as he gave Sevan a slight push toward them and as he turned to go back with the adults his eyes met with his wife's eyes and she was staring him with a side smirk on her face as she cut her eyes at him. No one in the room but Trey and his father caught their stares.

As they showed the last few guests out Sevan snuck and had a few more shots because the time was coming near that her father would surprise her with something *he* feels would make her have the "best birthday ever".

Sevan stood by the door as they waved off the last few people and as her mother closed the door her happy face that she had plastered on the entire evening disappeared.

"Could you be a little less obvious at the next party?" she started with Jonathan as he loosened his top button collar to his Ralph Lauren Polo shirt.

Jonathan knew she was going to start a fight with him and he was glad so that he could have an excuse to sleep in the guest room tonight. Sevan was looking more and more attractive to him and he wanted to show her how much she belonged to him and him only tonight.

He saw the way she and Trey were feeling each other, and he refused to let anyone else be her first after he had spent years building her up to this point.

"I'm not doing this with you tonight, Gianni," he said as he turned to head up the stairs.

"You will, Jonathan! You will do this with me and you listen to me because *I am* your wife!" she said as she followed behind him stomping her feet demanding to be heard.

"Go take a shower and get ready for bed." He said looking at Sevan.

She knew that meant get cleaned up because he was coming in there tonight. Sevan quietly followed behind the both slowly, as her father kept walking and her mother continued to yell.

"You don't think people noticed how you treat your little girl friend?" she yelled as if Sevan wasn't standing there.

Jonathan reached the top of the stairs and turned to look at her and she stopped a few steps down looking up at him fearing what he might do next since he had the advantage over her right now.

"I told you, I – am – not- doing – this – with- you! You and your crazy allegations about me and my daughter are getting old and I'm sick of it!"

So, she does know? Sevan thought to herself. If she knows why isn't she like other mothers? Why wouldn't she protect her from this monster?

"It's not crazy," she said softly almost to the point of tears. "I'm not crazy," she said as a tear escaped her left eye.

Jonathan shook his head and gave her a look of disgust. "Humph. Pitiful. I don't know why I even married your sorry black ass. The only thing you ever did right was give me Sevan."

He didn't bother to wait for her response, he turned and walked to the guest room. Sevan watched her mother freeze and she could tell that what he said had cut her deep. It hurt her to even hear him say something so cruel to her mother. In all the years she had never heard him be mean to her mother verbally.

Gianni took her left hand and grabbed the rail and held herself from falling backward for a moment as she stood there with her heart shattered in a million pieces. The only man she had ever loved, slept with, wanted to be with had just reminded her why she hated her black skin. She took her right hand and put it over her stomach when a sick feeling crept over her.

She stood there and had a quick flash back as to when he didn't talk to her like that. When he loved her, and desired her all the time. She thought about all the times they made love and all six of the pregnancies she had lost before they finally had Sevan, which is why she is named Sevan, she is the seventh child and he always said she was lucky number seven for them. That wasn't the same man who cleaned up her pool of blood from all of her horrible and painful miscarriages. He wasn't the same man she stood before God promising to love her forever. She didn't know who this monster was.

Sevan for the first time could feel her mother's pain and wanted so desperately to hug and say let's just leave! Let's run far away from him and never come back, but because she didn't have a bond with her she didn't know what to say or even how to say it.

Jonathan saw Sevan was still standing on the steps behind her and didn't like it. "Sevan, I will not repeat myself."

Sevan glanced up to the landing where he was as he gave her a look and she nodded back to him. "Yes, Daddy."

He walked in the guest room to go take a shower and closed the door behind him. Sevan touched her mother's shoulder gently.

Gianni turned to her and the tears poured as soon as she felt her touch. "Mommy, can I sleep with you tonight?"

Gianni stopped crying and looked into Sevan's eyes. For the first time they were both feeling desperate. She was desperate for her husband to desire her and Sevan was desperate to be freed from him.

Gianni stared into Sevan's eyes and she stopped crying. She could see the fear in her daughter's eyes and she glanced back to the guest room door and then back to Sevan. Jonathan had been sleeping in the guest room often the last few years and she always had an assumption as to what he was doing, and she knew now that she wasn't crazy. Sevan could tell her mother had figured it out and she felt like she might finally be free from it as they gazed into each other's eyes.

Gianni stopped her tears completely and her face turned cold out of nowhere. "No. Sleep in your own bed."

Sevan could feel her heart explode inside of her chest. What kind of mother would knowingly allow this to go on? She realized then that her mother resented her, and she was okay with the abuse and damage he was doing to her. Gianni turned and switched her way to her bedroom feeling like Sevan was going to get what she deserved.

Sevan didn't move as she stood frozen on the steps knowing there wasn't anyone coming to her rescue and it was time for her to walk that walk and take what was coming to her. As she slowly walked to the bathroom to shower she felt completely dead inside and numb. The shower was only ten minutes long, but it felt longer as she let the water run over her hair. Jonathan loved when her hair was wet and curly. She didn't want to upset him anymore than he was, so she made sure to lotion up in his favorite Bath and Body Works Moonlight Path and towel dried her hair so that the water would stop dripping down her neck.

She walked into her bedroom and slipped on her t-shirt and lay in the bed and prayed to God one more time. *If you don't stop this tonight I am convinced that you don't exist.*

She glanced at the clock after laying there staring at the ceiling as time was going by. It was now 3:15 am and he still hadn't come in there. She closed her eyes thinking maybe this time God had finally heard her and dozed off. After she finally allowed herself to sleep she felt his hands run up her thighs softly. The touch woke her up quickly and she immediately cursed God.

"You smell so good," he whispered.

She just stared trying to mentally prepare herself for what he was going to do. He took her cover and pulled it all the way off and slid her t-shirt up to make sure she was naked like he instructed her to do the nights he was coming to lay with her.

He smiled at her body. "This is what a real woman looks like," he whispered.

He took his hands and spread her legs and dived in face first. Usually he was gentle and slow, but today he didn't care. Her body jerked at the kisses, but her mind and soul screamed in agony. Jonathan stood up and was completely naked. He started to touch himself in front of her to make his erection harder.

"I can't wait to see if you feel as good as you taste," he moaned.

She knew he was going to penetrate her now and her heart began to race, and her head started hurting. She felt herself having a panic attack inside and didn't know what to do. She wanted to scream, but knew there was no point. Her own mother was in the next room and made it very clear that she wasn't coming to help her.

Jonathan slipped on a condom and laid on top of her and rubbed her hair gently. "I love you, Sevan."

She couldn't say it back to him. She didn't love him anymore and she didn't want to lie anymore. The pain in her head increased as she felt him move inside of her slowly. Her body jerked, and he thrust himself inside of her deeper and she felt a sudden pop inside of her vagina and inside of her head.

The pain in her head was so strong that she felt like her soul lifted out of her and was floating over the bed watching this man kill the rest of her childhood because of his sick desires. It seemed like hours that he was inside of her, but in reality, it was only ten minutes. Ten minutes that changed her life forever. Ten minutes that she would have gladly traded for death.

After he finished he didn't hold her like he usually does. He stood straight up next to the bed naked as he shook his head at her in disgust with the condom still hanging. She didn't move as she watched herself from above the bed lay there lifeless.

"Such a slut just like your mother. Clean yourself up," he sneered, as he walked out of the room naked and closed the door behind him.

Uncontrollable tears streamed Sevan's face as she held her face with both hands, crying as she relived that day. Steve wanted so bad to get up and hug her after she shared that piece of her life with him, but he knew that would be inappropriate and she wouldn't allow a man to touch her right now anyway.

He wanted to ask her about the pain she felt in her head as it went on to be sure he wasn't dealing with more than a molestation case, so he jotted down a reminder to ask her about it once she calmed herself. He thought it was interesting how she described seeing it from above her bed and not being there inside of her body, so he jotted a reminder to ask her about that as well.

He reached over to hand her the box of tissue and she jumped when she saw him coming closer to her, then relaxed when she saw he just wanted to give her the Kleenex.

"Why? Why does God hate me so much that he let them treat me like that?" she asked Steve through tears.

He didn't want the session to turn into a religious session, but he didn't want to not be able to give her an answer either.

"I don't think He hates anyone. I think sometimes He uses us so that His glory can be seen when He delivers us out of whatever hurt us."

Sevan stopped crying and sat up and placed her feet on the floor. "Bull shit. I don't even think He exists. I called on Him so many times! What did He deliver me from, Steve?"

Steve didn't know what to say. For the first time in his career he was at a loss for words.

"I don't know what His plan is for you, but you are here now. Maybe he sent you here, so he can work through me to

help you." Steve tried to find something to say that made sense.

Sevan smirked as the tears began to dry on her face. "You think **He** brought me here?"

Steve nodded. "Yes."

"Interesting," she said as she looked up in her head.

"Should we end for today or continue?" he asked.

"Since **GOD** brought me here, let's continue," she said as she laid back down.

"Can you tell me how your relationship with your mother was after that night?"

Just Us...

"I know you took it!" Gianni sneered in Sevan's face.

Sevan smirked and walked away toward the fridge as she reached in and grabbed some orange juice.

Gianni and Sevan had been nit picking at each other ever since her 16th birthday. Sevan had lost all respect for her mother after that night. She began to enjoy taunting her and making her feel inadequate as a woman. Jonathan was okay with it because it allowed him to be with them both freely now. He would still sneak, but they all knew what was going on.

Sevan had just come back from a 5-mile run, and she wasn't in the mood for Gianni. She began running more than often the last year and a half. She found it was a way to release some of the stress that she was feeling just breathing daily. She had sworn off that God existed and began to depend more on herself as her own savior.

"Oh, you feelin' yo' self, huh?" Gianni said, as she folded her arms across her chest and shifted her weight to her left leg.

Sevan stared her in the eyes as she took a sip of her orange juice.

"Been walkin' around her smellin' yourself, acting like your shit don't stink!" she continued.

Sevan knew she was agitating her, so she wanted to

continue. She sat her glass on the counter and slid her scrunchie off her hair and shook her head to let her curls fly free. She knew Gianni was jealous of her curly hair and she loved to see her face turn green with envy.

"I don't have a clue as to what you are talking about woman," she said taking her workout shirt off and tying it around her waist. She wanted to expose her perfect figure and navel ring she snuck off to get.

Gianni had no reason to be jealous of Sevan's figure because she was shaped the exact same way, but she was blinded by self-hatred ad she couldn't see how much her daughter resembled her, and the beauty she envied was the same beauty she possessed.

"Woman? You disrespectful little bitch!" she snapped.

Sevan laughed.

"I'm sorry, did you expect to be called Mommy?" she said as she placed her right hand on her hip.

Gianni uncrossed her arms and placed her left hand on her hip and pointed her right index finger toward her.

"I am your mother and you will address me as such!" she demanded.

"My mother? Tuh! Maybe you should have acted like it before we got to this point!"

Gianni had had more than enough of disrespect from Jonathan and she refused to take it from Sevan. She was beginning to feel like they were both against her and the only friend she had in their home now was Hennessey and depression pills.

The room became silent as they had a staring match. Sevan knew in her mind that Gianni was afraid of what her father would do to her so she wasn't worried about her physically touching her, until Gianni lunged at her and knocked her down and began to choke her.

"I hate you!" she screamed, through tears as saliva escaped her mouth splattering in Sevan's face.

"Get off of me!" Sevan screamed as she struggled to release the grip her mother had around her neck.

Sevan began kicking and wiggling her body to get her off of her but the more she squirmed the harder Gianni squeezed. Gianni began to feel herself enjoying the moment of possibly killing Sevan and tightened her grip.

"I should have aborted you so that Jon thought I had another miscarriage! We were happy until you came along!" she said staring her in the eyes.

Sevan felt herself becoming weak as she stared back into her mother's eyes. She swore the white part of her eyes disappeared making her entire eye seem completely black; almost demonic.

She couldn't take any more of the choking and decided to stop trying to pull her hands off of her neck and punch her mother in the face until she got off of her. She hit her with her right fist repeatedly, but it was like Gianni didn't feel it at all. The harder she hit her the tighter she squeezed.

Sevan couldn't fight her off anymore and the light began to fade to black and her body felt limp as she dropped her arms to her side and her head fell back and everything was dark.

When she awoke she was laying in her bed and her father was lying next to her. She jumped up and she could feel the pains in her neck from where she was choked. Her father was asleep, and she looked under the covers and she was naked. *Did this sick fuck have sex with me while I was passed out?*

She looked over at the clock and it was 3a.m.; the time he always came in her bedroom. She wondered how she had gotten in her bed because she thought her mother had killed her in the kitchen earlier that day.

Jonathon felt her move and he woke up and reached his left hand for her to come back to the bed.

"Hey, how you are feeling?" he asked sounding concerned.

She didn't say anything she just stood there naked rubbing her neck.

"I sent her away for a while. She won't be hurting you again." He said without Sevan saying anything.

Sevan didn't want her mother to be gone. Even though

they were at odds every day, her presence is what kept her father from being so free with his behavior as if they were a couple. He would have never slept in the bed with Sevan as he was doing so right now.

Sevan still didn't move. She just stared at him as her heart began to race at the thoughts of what he would be doing to her while she was "away".

"I told you I wouldn't let anyone hurt you ever." He assured her as he extended his hand some more. This time he gave her a look as if it wasn't an option to come back to bed, she was commanded to.

Sevan walked over to the bed and placed her hand in his as she laid back in the bed with her back to him. He pulled her closer so that they could spoon. As soon as his skin touched hers she closed her eyes and cringed. The touch of a man the way he held her would have soothed a woman in love; but she wasn't a woman in love. She wasn't even a woman yet.

To her surprise he wasn't erect, and he didn't attempt to have sex with her. All he did was cuddle. She was curious as to where he had "sent" her mother to.

"Dad?" she said softly because she wasn't sure if he dozed off.

"Yes?" he responded as his grip tightened on her.

"How long will Mom be gone?"

"Few weeks. Don't think about it. Let's just enjoy our

time alone," he said.

She knew that he was enjoying the fact that it would be just the two of them since school was out and she was gone. He said it as if it were their plan all along to eventually be alone together.

"Sevan, don't call me Dad when it's just us, ok?"

She didn't respond. He had forced her into a relationship she had no desire to be in. She hated that he had gotten rid of the live-in maids they had after she turned 13. He couldn't risk accidently being caught, so he made Gianni and Sevan keep up with the house.

Sevan closed her eyes after she realized she didn't have a choice anymore in the matter and hoped her dreams would take her far, far from where she was now. As soon as she closed her eyes she felt his right-hand slide between her legs. He couldn't see it, but tears began to slide down her face as she felt him began to massage her as he prepared to do what he always did.

She felt him lean closer as he became erect and more tears followed.

"You can be as loud as you want tonight...it's just us," he whispered in her ear, as if this was a treat.

Sevan knew she couldn't do anything but let him do what he wanted so she closed her eyes and began to visualize herself somewhere else. Once again, she felt her soul leave her body and levitate above the bed watching and crying for her as he had his way with her for the 227th time. 227 times that she had never asked for. 227 times of dying; even a cat only had nine lives.

She was now immortal in her mind. All she wanted was for her mother to come home. She would give anything to rewind the day and she wouldn't have pushed her to snap like she did. She would have backed down and let her win that round if she could go back in time. She knew the next few weeks alone would be hell for her.

"How long was she gone?" Steve asked.

Sevan wasn't crying when she told this piece of her life to him. She seemed to have went numb the more she talked. He knew she was reliving it all because of the great detail she shared with him.

"She was gone for a month," she replied angrily.

"A month?"

"Yes. A whole month. Jonathan didn't feel she was "better" yet so he kept her away."

"Why do you think he did that?"

Sevan cut her eyes at him. "I don't know Steve. Maybe because I got better at pleasing him and he didn't want it to end."

Steve didn't say anything. He didn't know what to say so he stayed quiet and jotted down what she said to him.

"I shouldn't have pushed her the way I did. I just was so sick of the arguing over a man I didn't want. I was so angry with her for knowing what he was doing and letting him do it."

"Yes, I can see that." Steve agreed to keep her talking. "How many times did he abuse you while she was gone?"

"Fifty. Fifty more times in one month. And each time he did he would buy me something. Probably to clear his conscious. The only thing he gave me that I liked was a Poodle."

"He bought you a pet?"

Sevan smiled at the thought of the gift. "Yes. Cherry. He named her that."

"Did you care for Cherry?"

Sevan laughed. "Sure, Steve."

Steve knew from her laugh there was something behind the laugh. It was an evil sinister laugh that gave him chills.

"Can you tell me about Cherry?" He decided to dig a little.

"Sure, Steve."

Cherry

"You should wear this dress instead." Jonathan said as he held up a white floral spaghetti strapped Dolce & Gabbana sun dress.

Sevan turned toward the door as she stood there in her panties and bra while she lotioned her body. Jonathan made her get dressed with the door open so that he could freely watch her whenever he pleased. The dress was ugly to her and looked more like something her mother would love.

At times she felt like he was trying to make her be like her mother. For example, he would bring in her mother's favorite movies for them to watch together or get her the ice cream her mother loved. She wondered why he just didn't do this for Gianni instead.

The one thing he gave her that he would never give her mother was a puppy. After Sevan slipped on the dress her father reached on the side of him on the floor outside of her bedroom door and handed her a white poodle puppy.

Sevan's heart jumped, and her face lit up. She hadn't smiled that big in a long time. Jonathan started smiling too because he had been trying to make her smile like this for the past few weeks and not one of his gifts phased her, except the poodle.

"Daddy!" she screamed, as she cuddled the puppy.

Jonathan didn't respond as he slid his hands in his pockets.

"Her name is Cherry," he said as he watched her enjoy his gift to her.

"She's beautiful!" she said as she continued to hug the wiggly puppy.

"You want to catch a movie?" he asked.

Sevan paused. She didn't want to go anywhere with him, but she knew she couldn't turn him down after he gave her a puppy.

"Sure, Da- Jonathan," she said, as she corrected herself.

He smiled. "Put the puppy outside in the cage near the garage and meet me in the car." He instructed as he walked out of her room without waiting for a response.

Sevan rolled her eyes and slowly followed behind so that she could spend more time with the puppy. For the first time since her 13th birthday she felt close to something. As she placed the puppy in the cage next to the garage she smiled as she watched how the poodle jumped toward her as they looked at each other. She touched the top of the cage and Cherry licked her hand. She smiled.

"Let's go, I don't want to miss the opening credits." Jonathan interrupted.

Sevan's smile disappeared as her back was still to him. "Coming."

He took her to a movie theater about an hour away from where they lived. She knew it was because he didn't want anyone to notice him and pick up on how she was dressed like a grown woman and then ask him questions about where Gianni was.

Her father held so much power it scared her. He somehow was able to get Gianni away for over a month without her losing her position at Cleveland General Hospital. She wondered how he even pulled something like this off.

During the movie he was the perfect gentleman and never touched her. He never even came close to attempting to sneak. Sevan relaxed and enjoyed herself since she didn't have to be on guard. She was hoping maybe he had grown tired of her since they had been under each other so much the last month.

On the way home he tried to make small talk.

"Did you like the movie?" he asked never taking his eyes off the road.

Sevan didn't respond because she was mesmerized with the sunset. She pictured herself flying away into it and disappearing like when she felt her soul leave her body. The thought made her smile.

"Sevan?"

"Hmm?" she said still staring as the sun continued to disappear.

"I asked if you enjoyed the movie."

"Oh. Yeah. *Dead Pool* was cool. Humorous," she said, hoping he would leave her to her fantasy.

"Are you hungry?"

She shook her head and folded her arms. She decided to play tired in hopes he would let her body rest tonight.

"No, just really tired."

He laughed. "You're too young to be tired."

That's when it dawned on her that it was her youth he was attracted to. He must have saw the young Gianni in her and that's what enticed him.

"Well, I am," she said, trying to sound serious.

Jonathan turned to her and his smile disappeared. She sounded just like her mother when she responded. He hated the tone in her voice and just as he was comfortable with her she had become comfortable with him enough to snap at him.

All of the charm Jonathan had for her that day disappeared that instant and his speed picked up. She wasn't sure what he was thinking, but could sense the vibe was off now and she regretted her comment and tone.

They seemed to have reached home faster than when they were on their way to the movies. When they got there, he pulled into the garage and closed it quickly. Her heart beat picked up and her palms started to sweat. She knew something was wrong.

"Jonathan, I'm sorry, I didn't mean to snap. I'm just so tired," she began, as she turned in her seat to face him.

He stared at her with disgust. "I buy you a pretty dress, get you a puppy, and take you out, and this is how you treat me?" he started.

His tone was so different, almost the same tone he used with her mother and at that moment she feared him.

"I'm sorry. It won't happen again," she tried to assure him.

There was complete silence between them and he unzipped his pants. Tears streamed her face immediately.

"Jonathan, no, please," she begged.

She hated performing oral on him more than actual sex.

It was like he enjoyed her crying and the power he held over her right now. He grabbed the back of her hair and titled her head back as she continued to cry looking him in his eyes. She hoped that him seeing the pain he was causing her right now would make him feel some sympathy and stop, but it just fueled him.

"Shut up," he snapped. "I'll show you how to use your mouth the right way!"

He shoved her head in his lap and for the next 6 ½ minutes she watched herself die again. She watched him kill her over and over again from above her body.

When he was done he mugged her head off of him and zipped his pants up.

"Next time I better cum in three minutes," he said as he got out the car and slammed the door.

Sevan didn't move. She watched him go into the door that led to the kitchen and slam it. She sat there crying and screaming alone as she hit the dashboard over and over with her fist. Usually when he was done her soul would return to her and she would face reality. This time she felt herself still watching her as she screamed how she can't take this anymore.

She jumped out of the car and slammed the door and leaned against the car, breathing and panting heavy as her tears began to dry up and she began to feel anger, an uncontrollable anger. She balled her fist up and started looking around the garage. She walked over to her father's tool table and saw some metal scissors and picked them up.

She looked up over her as if she could see her soul looking at her and she could see it as well. She walked outside the garage where Cherry's cage was and grabbed the cage. Cherry was excited to see her new master as she carried her into the backyard near the woods.

Sevan glanced up as she noticed the moon was full and she could feel her soul following over her in the night. She paused and dropped the cage as she kneeled down and pulled Cherry out.

Cherry jumped into her arms and began to lick her and kiss her. Sevan couldn't feel the same feeling that she felt when she first met Cherry. She didn't feel anything at all right now. She took Cherry and pulled her head the way her father had just pulled hers in the car. The puppy began to make soft noises of pain.

Sevan grinned as she looked into the puppy's eyes and began to stab the puppy with the scissors until she no longer could see white; until she was completely covered in blood. At that moment she looked up into the moon again as she took a deep breath and inhaled deeply, as if she were intaking her soul in as she felt her body relax and she stood up with the scissors still in her hand as she walked back to the garage to clean them off.

Steve didn't say a word after she told him what she had done. He couldn't move or write any notes. He was in complete shock as he stared at her realizing that he was dealing with more than child molestation. He didn't know if he should end the session for the day or continue. His heart was racing, and he was honestly afraid to ask any more questions.

Sevan felt his change and sat up straight and placed her feet on the floor, so she could look him in his eyes.

"Did I scare you, Steve?" she calmly asked.

He lied. "No."

"Not at all, Steve?" she pushed.

He shook his head as he tried to force himself to get back into treating her. She laughed.

"It's okay if I did, Steve. I scared myself telling you that. You know something, I never told anyone what happened to Cherry, but you."

"Your father never asked?" he asked surprised.

She shook her head. "I think he knew when he found the dress in the trash covered in blood and the dog was found on one of his walks," she laughed.

"And he never mentioned it to you?"

She shook her head. "Steve, if you would have found an innocent puppy stabbed to death and the dress with the puppy's blood on it; how would you confront it?" she asked with a sly grin.

Steve paused. He really didn't know how he would confront something like that to his own daughter.

"I- I honestly don't know."

"Don't know how to or if you would?"

Steve paused before answering. "Either. I don't know what I would say or do."

She smiled and leaned her back against the couch.

"Did you enjoy it?"

"Which part?"

"Any of it. Did you enjoy killing the puppy?"

She nodded. "I enjoyed it so much that I knew then what I

wanted to do with my life."

Steve was afraid to ask what that was, so he didn't interrupt he just allowed her to talk.

She could sense she was scaring him, so she backed down some.

"I knew I wanted to be in the medical field."

He took a sigh of relief and hoped that was the only thing she realized. He knew that sociopaths often started killing with animals first.

"What did you want to do in the medical field?"

She shrugged. *"Anything that involved using a scalpel."*

Steve immediately jotted down notes about her body language that she was displaying right now. He was becoming afraid and intrigued at the same time. So much that even after two hours in he needed to hear more.

"I need to change the tape."

She nodded. *"Go ahead. I have more to tell you."*

Steve jumped up and ran to the office where his assistant usually is at and scrambled through the drawers looking for the pack of tapes he asked her to pick up and ran back in to the room.

"Steve, where on earth did you find these?" she asked as she grabbed the two packs of mini tapes while he changed it.

"It's hard to find," he said not looking her way.

"You do know that they have them digital now right?" she teased.

He nodded. "Yes, but I like doing it the way my father did." He regretted mentioning that to her right after he said it.

"Your father?" she asked.

"Uh, yeah. This was his practice. He passed a few months ago. We worked side by side."

"How did he die?" she asked.

"Someone murdered him," he sadly said.

"Oh no! Were they caught?"

He shook his head sadly. "No."

"That's terrible." She sounded concerned.

"Can we continue?" he asked, changing the subject.

She nodded.

"So, you decided to go into the medical field?"

She nodded.

I want to be just like you!

"Sevan, get the door for your mother." Jonathan instructed as he pulled in the driveway with Gianni.

Sevan was happy to see her even though the terms of her being gone was bad between them. She couldn't hide it either.

Gianni turned her head to look at Jonathan as he sat and waited for Sevan with his foot on the brake. He wasn't as thrilled for Gianni to be home as Sevan was. He enjoyed having peace in the house. Gianni would talk back to Jonathon and raise hell whenever she felt like it; whereas he controlled Sevan completely.

Gianni wanted to say something slick to him about him telling her to help her out of the car, but she was afraid he would send her back to the crazy house for another month. She honestly didn't know how he was able to send her away for so long and keep it from Cleveland General Hospital so that she could keep her job.

She slowly slid out of the car as Sevan stood there anticipating seeing her face to face. As soon as she closed the passenger door behind her Jonathan pulled off and went to the garage. Sevan moved in close to her mother as they stared into each other's eyes.

Even though Gianni had hatred for Sevan buried deep to her core, for some reason at the moment they locked eyes she didn't feel that hate rise. Instead she felt the feeling she felt when she first gave birth to Sevan. The emotions of when a mother first sees her child and holds her baby for the first time began to surface.

Sevan could feel her energy and thought that what she was feeling looking at her mother was mutual, and she reached in quickly and hugged her tight. The tighter she hugged she began to close her eyes and enjoy the moment. A moment she dreamed of since she was a little girl.

Gianni couldn't help but to embrace her back because she too desired to feel comfort and love like this especially being alone for the last month. As she let herself enjoy the moment she felt a sudden shift in her emotions and felt as if she were being embraced not by her own daughter, but her husband's mistress. The thoughts she had when she was away came right back; thoughts that they planned for her to be gone just so they could be alone together, and she started to feel rage instantly.

Gianni suddenly snatched away from Sevan and stared her in the eyes again. This time her eyes returned to the Gianni Sevan remembered and she knew that nothing would change. She knew then that they would be at odds like they were before she left. She hoped that maybe she could change that. Anything to save their relationship and perhaps save her from Jonathan.

"How are you feeling…..Mommy?" Sevan pushed out. Gianni wasn't the only one that had a hard time coping with their relationship.

Gianni paused as she attempted to read Sevan. She

never could. She never could figure her out or what she thought.

"I'm ok," she responded dryly.

Sevan smiled as she held both of her mother's hands with a small grip so that she couldn't easily pull away.

"Well, I've missed you. Where did you go?" Sevan hoped her mother would tell her before her father walked up.

Gianni squinted her eyes. She was beginning to believe Sevan was playing games with her. She had to have known where he sent her. She wasn't about to fall into the trap for Sevan's amusement.

"Are you being funny?" she asked.

Sevan stopped smiling and had a confused look on her face.

"What? No."

"Hmmm. You know where I went. Wasn't it part of you two little plan to get me out of the house so that you could be together?" she said as she jerked her hands from the grip Sevan attempted to keep and folded them across her chest.

"What? No!" she began to get agitated at the accusations then quickly stopped herself so that he wouldn't send her away again.

"Mom, I had nothing to do with that. Look I don't want

to fight anymore, ok?" she sounded as sincere as she could hoping her mother could read it.

Gianni relaxed her attitude and her shoulders followed. She wanted to let her guards down, but her pride wouldn't let her.

Sevan extended her left hand to Gianni and she slowly extended her right hand and locked hands with hers as they walked in the house. Gianni wanted to fight it, but she couldn't. Just as bad as Sevan needed this so did she.

When they walked inside the house Gianni paused by the front door and looked around. She began to have flashbacks of the painful memories the house held. She looked up at the top of the stairs where she remembered Jonathan saying how he didn't know why he even married her black ass. She closed her eyes as she heard his voice saying it in her mind and felt a pain reenter her heart.

She opened her eyes and looked toward the landing and her eyes landed on the guest room door. She stared at it thinking about how he would creep in there at night. How he would start fights with her to sleep in there so that he could be with Sevan. She felt her heart breaking slightly and wanted to cry, but knew it wouldn't do any good.

Jonathan walked in behind her and the slam of the front door scared her slightly. He stood next to her and looked to where her eyes moved as he placed his right hand in the small of her back. His touch used to be so soft and comforting; right now, it only made her cringe.

"Everything is still the way you left it," he assured her.

"Hmmm." she said thinking how she didn't want her life to be the way she left it. She needed it to change.

"Listen, I have to go out of town for a few days. Should I take Sevan or will you two be ok?" he asked hoping she said take her with him.

Sevan heard what he said, and she felt sick inside hoping and praying her mother would say she could stay with her. She was in eye sight of her mother while her father's back was to her. She stared Gianni in the eyes with the hopes she could read her eyes that were begging her to say she could stay with her.

Gianni paused for a moment and turned to face Jonathan with a side grin. "No, Love. She can stay home with me."

For the first time in her life she felt like her mother might be on her side. She noticed the facial expression she gave, but she felt like anything would be better than being alone with him again.

Jonathan paused as he stared Gianni in her eyes. She was beautiful. He hadn't noticed how she aged so gracefully until now because he was taken by Sevan's youthful beauty. He leaned in and kissed her lips softly as he closed his eyes to embrace the moment. Gianni closed hers after a moment and began to return the kiss.

As much as Sevan wanted this to happen so that he would leave her alone, for some reason she felt sick in her stomach seeing it and envy began to rise in her. She didn't even know why she felt envious she just knew she did. She turned her head and looked away as she questioned herself internally as to why she felt like that.

Jonathan pulled away from the kiss and placed his right hand on Gianni's cheek as she opened her eyes and smiled. She longed for that moment for the last six years. She missed them kissing and hugging all the time.

"When are you leaving?" she asked softly.

"Now. I just wanted to get you settled first," he said in his most caring voice.

"Ok."

"Gianni?" he said as he moved closer to her.

"Yes?" she responded, as her heart beat faster.

"I love you, okay?"

She closed her eyes as she took in what he just said. She hadn't heard those words from him in years and she hadn't felt love from him.

"I love you, Jonathan."

He kissed her forehead and turned to leave, and Sevan was staring him in his eyes. She had fury in her eyes. She didn't even look like herself. She was looking at him how Gianni used to look at him when he would interact with Sevan. He felt like he was caught between two women right now, but knew there wasn't anything Sevan could say.

Sevan still hadn't a clue as to why she was feeling like that, but she felt like she wanted to punch him in his mouth. Her heart beat picked up and she felt rage inside of her. She felt like she did the night she killed Cherry. *You put me through all of this just to be back in love with her?*

Jonathan felt his face get flushed as he felt the energy coming from Sevan. Gianni couldn't see her facial expressions because she was directly behind Jonathan.

"Sevan, have fun with your mother," he said, and walked out of the house.

She took a deep breath and released the energy she had and felt her body temperature return to normal.

There was silence as the two of them stared at each other. They were left in the house together alone for the first time since the fight, and it was like they were strangers meeting for the first time.

"Now what?" Sevan asked breaking the silence.

"How long is he supposed to be gone?"

Sevan shrugged. "I didn't even know he was leaving until now."

Gianni nodded as she folded her arms and looked around. "Hmm. Well first things first, we are getting rid of that guest room."

Sevan smiled. She knew that was the key to him having access to her freely and she was about to take it away.

"You like to work out, right?" she asked Sevan.

"Yes."

"Okay, let's turn it into a workout room. We don't need a guest room anyway. We never have guest," Gianni said as she headed up the stairs.

After Jonathan kissed her she believed there was hope for her marriage after all. She tried to bury the thoughts of Sevan and Jonathan really being together. She tried to convince herself that she was just paranoid and that really couldn't happen. She knew Jonathan and she knew he couldn't do something so sick, right?

Sevan followed behind her excited about what they were about to do, together.

"Hey, Mom?" Sevan asked as they entered the room.

"What's up?" Gianni asked, as she looked around the bedroom trying to figure out what she was going to do.

"I was thinking while you were away. I'd like to go to school for nursing, maybe even become a doctor."

Gianni paused and gave Sevan her full attention. "Really?"

She nodded. "Yeah. I want to be just like you."

"Did you mean that? When you told her that you wanted to

be just like her? Or were you trying to establish a relationship you never had with her?" Steve asked.

Sevan smirked as she sat up again to look Steve in his eyes. "I meant it."

Steve nodded. "Okay. How do you think she felt when she heard it?"

Sevan shrugged. "She seemed excited about it. It was all she talked about for days after I told her that."

"What was your father's response about the bedroom being changed into a work out area?"

Sevan dropped her head. "He may as well have killed us both. He didn't see it for about 2 weeks."

"Two weeks? He didn't notice an entire room was changed for two weeks?" Steve asked in disbelief.

"That's how long it took before he decided he wanted to sleep with me again."

Steve frowned. "What did he say when he saw the room?"

Sevan lay back on the couch and stared at the mural again.

Ivy Lee

Work it out!

"Sevan, after we put the bags away, do you want to get a quick work out in with me?" Gianni asked, as she and Sevan entered the house from shopping all day at the mall together.

Since Gianni came home she and Sevan had been spending every day together. Jonathan stayed out of Sevan's room. He didn't even look her way. He had been so into Gianni the last few weeks and things seem to appear how a normal family would be.

"Yeah," Sevan said excitedly. She really didn't feel like working out after all the walking and shopping and eating they were doing, but she refused to pass up a chance to do anything with her mother.

Gianni smiled and nodded her head as she walked to her room to change and put her bags away. The fall weather was coming faster than normal in Cleveland and she felt herself feeling sick from the weather change and wanted to try and sweat it out before the sickness kicked in.

Sevan raced to her room and threw on her *PINK* by Victoria Secret workout clothes. She was enjoying the new-found friendship she and her mother were building.

She hurried down the hall with one tennis shoe in her hand and the other on her foot with the laces untied. She didn't know why she ran down there without getting dressed as if her mother was going to pull off and leave her.

Gianni and Sevan made the room into an entire gym. Gianni had full wall mirrors installed on two of the walls. She had a treadmill, stair master and an elliptical for cardio workouts. Against one wall there were shelves of weights and exercise balls.

She ordered a *Bow-flex* home gym for the toning. In the corner by the door she put a mini stainless-steel fridge that she filled with water and Gatorades. On one half of the room there was padded mats for floor workouts.

Sevan walked in and sat on the weight bench and began to fix her laces and put on her other shoe. Gianni walked in behind her and closed the door as she took her hair and put it in a ponytail while she walked toward the sound bar to turn the music on.

"Who are we working out to today?" Gianni asked as she looked through the Pandora station on the iPod.

Sevan stood up and began to tie her hair into a bun on her head. "Go to the Missy Elliot station. She always has music that makes you want to move."

Gianni laughed. "Yeah, she does. Missy it is!"

As soon as she hit play on the station the beat dropped, and the song began; *Music make you lose control, music make you lose control……*

Gianni began to bob her head and face the mirror and Sevan followed suite. The more the song went on the more they got into it and Gianni lead the workout with jumping jacks for the next three minutes as Sevan followed.

As they stared at themselves in the mirror staying on beat with the music and each other, the next song up was Chingy *Right Thurr* and Sevan paused.

"Uh, Uh! What is this? Skip!" she yelled laughing.

Gianni stopped and faced her and giggled. "Oh, you don't know about this huh?"

Gianni began to move her right leg to the front and switched legs as she moved her arms with it doing the dance that was made for the song. The more she danced and sang the song and moved her hips the more Sevan laughed because she hadn't see her mother like this since she was a kid.

"You can't be serious!" Sevan laughed.

"Come on, come do it with me." She said as she kept dancing.

Sevan watched the rhythm and joined in with her side by side as they laughed and danced together. Gianni began to turn in a circle as she did the dance and when she turned around Jonathan was standing there, furious.

Gianni paused because she was unaware of what was wrong with him as she stood straight up and faced him. Sevan immediately shut the iPod off and waited for his response.

His face was blood red and his eyes were dark. They had never seen him like this before.

"Who told you to get rid of *MY* room?" he snarled.

Gianni looked over at Sevan then quickly back to him. "It's the guest room and we never have guests, so I figured it would be nice to have a home gym."

"Did you ask me?" he said, gritting through his teeth.

Gianni paused and put her hand on her hip. 'I don't believe I need to ask you permission to do anything in this house."

He balled his fist up and his face was completely blood red now. He wasn't upset that they had a workout room. He was upset that they took away his reason to start a fight and sleep elsewhere so that he could be with Sevan.

"You think this is how you're gonna win her over, Gianni?" he asked her as he moved slowly toward her. "You think you can be a dead-beat mother her whole life and this will make her like you now?" he continued, as he waved his arms in reference to the room.

Gianni immediately became defensive. "Dead beat?"

"DEAD BEAT BITCH!" he screamed, as he grabbed one of the hand weights to the left of him and threw it in her direction.

Gianni screamed and ducked to the ground as the weight flew over her head just missing her and shattering one of the wall mirrors. Sevan gasped. She'd never seen them like this and she didn't know what to do. She knew that she would choose Gianni and have her back if needed, but at the moment she was just spectating.

"What the fuck is wrong with you Jonathan?!" she screamed.

The shattering of the glass must have fueled him because he took another weight and threw it and broke the other mirror.

At this time Sevan was frozen in place. She felt like her feet were held to the floor like cement; as if she were a permanent fixture of the room now. Tears began to slide down her cheek when the glass hit the floor. It was like everything was in slow motion now. Jonathan was now unstoppable.

After he threw the weight he walked over and yanked the sound bar off the wall and kicked the fridge over. He took a kettle bell weight and began to bang the treadmill with it until the computer in it shattered.

"Stop it! Stop it!" Gianni screamed, as she held her clenched fist by her side.

Jonathan dropped the weight and rushed over to her and knocked her down. She fell, and her left arm was cut on a piece of the mirror on the floor. She gasped as she grabbed her arm and pulled it across her body while the blood began to seep out.

Sevan's tears began to stream faster.

Jonathan knelt down and grabbed Gianni's pony tail and began to drag her toward the door. She tried to pull away but the pain from her cut began to burn as the blood was dripping on the floor and her clothes.

"Stop Jonathan! You're hurting me!" she begged.

Sevan was scared as she watched him drag her mother

closer to the door and she struggled to pull away with pieces of the broken mirror attached to her.

"Daddy," she said softly.

Jonathan paused in mid walk with his grip still tight on Gianni's pony tail and looked back toward Sevan. Something about her voice broke him out of his trance he was in.

"Please let her go. Please," she softly begged him.

Jonathan paused and released the grip he had on her hair.

"Clean this shit up," he commanded and walked out the room.

Sevan snatched her work out tank off and fell beside her mother and immediately wrapped her arm up to stop the bleeding. Gianni rested her head on Sevan's chest after she wrapped her arm as Sevan knelt beside her and just cried.

"It's okay, Mommy," she said, trying to soothe her mother as she cried with her.

Gianni hugged Sevan tighter and the tears poured faster.

Sevan sat up as she wiped tears from her face and reached for more tissue. Steve felt himself a little emotional after the great details she shared. He felt like he was present with them the way Sevan told the story.

"Why do you think he was so angry?" Steve asked.

"She took away his reason to sneak in the room with

me. He no longer had a reason to sleep away from their bedroom. He hated her for that," she said, as she wiped her tears.

"And how did you feel about what she did?"

"I love her for it. She saved me for two whole weeks. Two. It felt good to be able to sleep knowing that he wasn't going to bother me."

"After he damaged the entire room, did your mother give him back his guest room?"

Sevan shook her head. "No. She stood her ground. She had the mirrors replaced and everything put back the way it was. I admired her for that," she said, as she stared at the table with a slight smile.

"Where do you think her strength came from all of a sudden? She seemed to have been under his spell before, but now she became strong. Strong enough to fight for you."

"Her time away made her stronger. Whatever happened to her when she was away made her stronger."

"Would you like to stop for the day?"

"No."

"Okay. Tell me, after all of that and watching how you and your mother began to get closer, did he ever sexually molest you again?"

Sevan nodded. "Yep. Right before my high school graduation."

Steve's eyebrows raised. "What?"

It's your big day!

The alarm clock went off as Sevan stared at the ceiling. She glanced over at the clock as the sounds echoed in the air; 7:30am. It was time to get up, but she didn't budge. Today was her graduation day and she didn't feel as excited as she thought she would.

The alarm continued to buzz as she returned her focus back to the ceiling. Somehow, she was able to tune it out. All kind of thoughts ran through her mind; college, her father, her mother, meeting people outside of her family that she would be able to interact with like a normal person, feelings of failure; her mind raced until she began to feel anxiety.

Gianni burst open the door breaking her train of thought as she smacked the alarm clock to shut off the sound.

"Chile', you don't hear this? I hear it all the way down the hall!" she said putting her left diamond stud in as she stood over the bed staring Sevan in the face.

Sevan stayed lying on her back with her right arm behind her head propping her up slightly.

Gianni paused after screwing the back on her earring and had a look of concern on her face.

"What's wrong? It's your big day! Aren't you excited?" she said as she placed her hands on her hips.

Sevan didn't respond as she stared at her mother. She hadn't realized how beautiful she was in a long time. Gianni stood there with a royal blue Chanel blouse on with a black pencil skirt. She hadn't chosen her shoes just yet, but her hair was pinned up to expose her diamond earrings. Her make-up was almost like it didn't exist; she had it on so natural that it only enhanced her beauty.

There was silence between them as Gianni waited for her to respond and when she didn't she sat on the bed next to her and reached for her free hand.

"Sevan, what's the matter?" she asked again.

"I don't know."

"What do you mean you don't know? You're laying here with the alarm clock going off as if you don't hear it, you're staring at me like we just met. What's wrong?"

"I'm afraid."

Gianni looked puzzled. "Afraid of what?"

"Leaving. I don't know what else is out there. I know the demons here, but I don't know the ones out there."

Gianni sighed as she stared into her only child's eyes. She had no word for her. She couldn't lie to her and tell her life would be better for her away from there because she honestly didn't know. Jonathon had them locked away from the rest of the world so long that all they knew was each other.

"I think you will do fine. You survived here all your life, out there can't be much worse, can it?"

Sevan didn't say anything she just tightened the grip on Gianni's hand as she rolled onto her side.

"That's what scares me. Can life be worse out there than here?"

Gianni bit the inside of her jaw and looked away. She didn't know what to tell her and she couldn't come up with anything, so she just returned the grip.

"I think you will be a wonderful nurse, Sevan. Just go to school and focus on that. Your tuition is already paid for, you'll have a job at the Cleveland General Hospital as soon as you graduate. Everything that others have to worry about is already in place for you. Just stay focused."

Sevan nodded. "Okay."

"You will do fine. I'm not worried about you."

"I'm worried about you, though."

Gianni felt herself about to cry when she said that, and she quickly jumped up and went to door. "Ehh, don't worry about me. I got some tough skin," she said as she winked at her. "Now, get up! It's your big day!"

Sevan gave a half smile as Gianni closed the door behind her. She sat up and moved her legs close to her chest as she locked her hands around them and rested her chin on her knees.

It had been months since her father even looked her way. They hadn't spoken much after he did damage to the workout room. Most of the time he avoided her. She heard a knock on her door then it opened immediately after before she could say come in; it was Jonathan.

He walked in with a bouquet of pink roses and a half smile.

Sevan's facial expression matched his. She didn't want to give too much, and not too little, as to set him off.

"Hey," he said as she set the flowers on the bed beside her and slowly sat next to them. Out of instinct she gripped herself tighter.

"Hey."

"Excited about today?"

She shrugged. "A little."

"I didn't know what to get you for graduation, so I just got flowers."

"Thanks."

He nodded as he looked around her room. "Haven't been in here in a while."

Sevan squinted her eyes. She couldn't believe that he was talking to her the way he was right now.

"Have you missed me?" he said as he returned his attention back to her.

"What?" she asked confused.

"Have you missed me?" he asked, but this time he ran his fingertips across her arms.

She didn't respond. She began to wonder where her mother was since he felt so comfortable coming in her room right now.

"Where's Mom?" she blurted out.

He laughed. "Don't worry. She won't catch us. She left to get you a present," he said as he loosened the grip she had around her legs.

She began to feel sicker in her stomach. He thought she was worried about her catching them as if this is something she wanted and that scared her.

"Dad, please," she said as she tried to move away.

Jonathan ignored her as he grabbed her legs and moved her body closer to his.

"You always smell so good," he said, as he placed his face between her legs.

Sevan for the first time tried to push him off of her. "Stop! I don't want this!" she yelled.

Jonathan paused and moved back from her. He stood up and didn't say anything as he backed out of the room slowly.

Is this all it took?

He left the room without saying a word. She had never

rejected him before, and the way that he left she wished she had done that a long time ago. It was now 8:15 and she decided to get up to shower and get ready. She hurried down the hall to the bathroom and hopped in the shower.

As she let the water run over her face and hair she closed her eyes picturing what her life could be like; possibly normal. After she washed up and got out of the shower there was Jonathan standing there waiting for her.

"You fuckin' someone else?" he asked with his fist balled up to his side.

Sevan quickly wrapped the towel around her as her heart began to race.

"What?"

He moved closer. "I said are you fuckin' someone else?"

She shook her head slowly. "No."

"Don't fuckin' lie to me Sevan!" he yelled.

"I swear!" she yelled back to him.

He moved closer to her as she backed near the bathroom sink.

When he was about a few inches from her his facial expression had changed. "You are so beautiful."

Sevan tightened the towel. Jonathan paused as he had a softer look on his face than he had a few moments ago and in less than a minute it became aggressive as he grabbed her by her throat and threw her on the counter and spread he legs apart.

Sevan tried to fight him, but he was so much bigger and stronger than she was. He took his left hand and pulled his member out and thrust it inside of her as she cried, and he moaned.

"Please!" she begged.

"Ahhh, yeah, it's still mine!" he said, as he gripped her throat and continued to thrust deeper inside of her.

He loosened his grip as she could feel he was about to climax. Usually Sevan would blank out and she would feel like she was having an outer body experience and wouldn't feel what he was doing to her body; today was different. Today her soul had failed her. Today she felt every thrust, every grip, every part of his member and every kiss and lick he gave her face and neck as he raped her.

Usually Jonathan would pull out of her right before he ejaculated, but this time he pushed himself deeper inside of her and she could feel his semen inside her. She closed her eyes and cried from the feeling. He had completely lost himself this time.

She wondered where her mother was this time. She had been her savior since she came home from the hospital. Sevan couldn't figure out why he all of a sudden had an interest in her again since he had fallen in love with her mother again.

Jonathan pulled back after he released himself and wiped

the sweat from his brow as he stared at Sevan. She didn't move. She stared back at him as she felt her tears dry on her face. He glanced down between her legs and his eyes widened. She followed where he was looking at and there was a pool of blood on the sink and her inner thigh. He looked at himself and there was blood on him as well.

Sevan wiped herself with her right hand and there was more blood coming out of her and she panicked as she tried to stand up and used both hands to continue wiping herself to see how much blood was there.

"What did you do?" she whispered through tears, as she pulled the towel off of her completely and began to wipe herself some more.

The more she wiped the more the blood ran. Jonathan stood there scared and didn't respond as he watched her wipe the blood.

"Why...why am I bleeding like this?" she cried softly.

"I-I-I don't know," he said quietly as he stayed planted, watching her.

Sevan looked up as him as she noticed the blood wouldn't stop and she passed out on the floor.

"Why do you think he decided to rape me then, Steve?" Sevan asked.

She was sitting up with her knees touching as if she were trying to keep her legs closed; like she could remember the pain she felt as she shared yet another rape with him. Her feet were inward facing each other, and her knees were tight together. She was sitting up straight on the edge of the couch as she had her arms straight gripping the edge of the couch tightly with her elbows completely locked. Her body language told Steve she was reliving the moment, so he wanted to make sure he was as sensitive as he could be with her.

"I think he is just sick, Sevan."

Sevan stopped rocking and gave him a cold stare. "Sick?"

Steve nodded. "Yes."

"Sick? He is more than sick! Sick is when you can go get something to make you better, Steve. Tell me, what can make a perverted rapist ass pedophile better Steve? What's the cure for that?"

Steve didn't respond. He could sense her anger and decided to digress.

"I'll tell you what the cure is, Steve. It's death."

Steve's eyes widened. "Is he dead, Sevan?" he was afraid to ask.

She laughed when she saw his facial expression. "Not literally, Steve. But he has died plenty of times."

Steve was confused as to who he was dealing with now at this point. Sevan's moods, facial expressions, body language and voice tones had changed so much during this session it scared him.

"I don't understand."

"Just stay with me, Steve. We're getting there."

Steve paused and wondered if he should end the session, but his curiosity was getting the best of him.

"Okay, please continue."

College Life

"Sevan!" Ryan called out.

Ryan was Sevan's college roommate at Ursuline College. Time literally flew by for Sevan as she made it to her last year of college. She enjoyed every bit of living on campus and away from home. Her new-found freedom was everything she could imagine. She would go home only on holidays, but had lunch with her mother quite often since her school was in Cleveland still.

"Sevan!" Ryan yelled again, this time nudging her to wake her up.

Ryan was about 5'7" with a caramel skin. She had an athletic build because she ran track and kept her hair cut short like Rhianna. She didn't have any features that stood out; just a killer body. She was just the girl next door. She was also in school to be a nurse practitioner just like Sevan, so they often did all of their work together. I guess you could say they were best friends, or as close to one as Sevan would ever have.

"Go away, Ryan. I'm exhausted," Sevan said as she turned over and placed the pillow over her face.

"Aren't we all?" she replied as she snatched the pillow off of Sevan's face and threw it across the room. "Now get up! We're almost done with this shit, don't mess up now." She said as she walked back to her side of the room and put on her jogging pants.

"Uuuuuhhh!" Sevan yelled as she stomped out of the bed.

Even though Ryan got on her nerves, Sevan appreciated how she kept her on her toes. There were plenty of days she just wanted to quit, then she would remember about having to go back home to her father's house and Ryan would talk her out of quitting school.

"I think you need some fun." Ryan suggested.

Sevan walked into the bathroom ignoring her as she grabbed her toothbrush.

Ryan walked over to the desk and sat down and quickly opened her laptop to check her Facebook account.

"There's a party tomorrow night. We should go," she yelled to her.

Sevan walked out to face her as she continued to brush her teeth with her hair everywhere and an oversized Ursuline t-shirt on. She gave Ryan a *now you know I'm not going to no party* look.

Ryan glanced up at her then back to the computer. "I don't care about your faces. I just told them we'll be there."

Sevan walked back in the bathroom and rinsed her mouth quickly to come back and yell at Ryan.

"Ryan, I am not goin'!"

Ryan rolled her eye and shut her laptop as she jumped up and put her books in her backpack. "Yeah you are. Now hurry up. You're about to be late. I'm going to the cafeteria and I'll see you in class."

Ryan walked out without waiting for a response from Sevan. Just as the door shut Sevan's cell rang. Her home number flashed across the screen and she smile when she knew her mother was calling.

"Hey, Ma," she said in a pleasant voice.

"It's your father."

She paused. He never calls her. Ever. They hadn't talked since the rape in the bathroom. When she would come home from school he would always be away for a business trip conveniently. She never told her mother what happened either.

"Hey." Her voice dimmed.

"How are you?" he asked.

She wondered why the phone call, then she began to panic thinking something was wrong with her mother. "Is something wrong with Mom?"

"What? No. Nothing is wrong with her."

She took a sigh of relief.

"I just wanted to check on you. Hear your voice. I was on your Facebook and saw how much of a beautiful woman you are becoming and thought I would call."

Sevan cringed inside. She hated when he told her she was beautiful. She knew that if he had saw her pictures and if she were around he would gladly show her how beautiful he thought she was. Everything inside her began to feel dead again; like when she lived with him. Just hearing his voice and how he was talking so smooth as if he never did anything to hurt her made her angry.

"Sevan?"

"I'm here," her tone was like ice.

"Do you miss me?" he asked with his voice getting lower.

"Do I what?" she snapped.

"Tell me you miss me," he whispered.

His voice sounded as if he were talking on the phone to sex hotline. She didn't answer.

"I miss you," he moaned slightly.

"What are you doing?" she asked hoping she wasn't hearing what she thought she was hearing.

"Looking at your pictures. Wondering if *it's* still the same," he whispered.

"What the fuck is wrong with you?!" she screamed and threw her cell across the room.

She became so angry that she started pacing back and forth. All the memories of what went on began to swim through her head. The more she remembered the faster she paced and the tighter her fist became.

The feeling that she got when her head would hurt and she

felt like her soul left her body began to come over her. As she felt herself levitate into the air she began to go numb and her body shut down. She sat at the desk Ryan sat at to go shut down her Facebook account so that he couldn't see her any longer. As soon as she logged on a sponsored site popped in her feed about meeting local singles in her area and the picture of the person used for the advertisement looked exactly like a younger version of her father. Same hair style and color. His eyes were similar and so was his smile.

Sevan, still feeling numb inside as her soul watched over her, she paused and stared at the picture for a few minutes and decided to click on the link. As soon as she did it redirected her from Facebook and took her to the site to sign up as a single looking for singles in her area. She didn't want just any single to link with though; she wanted the man on the advertisement that brought her to this site; or at least someone that looked like him.

She continued putting in information that was asked; Woman seeking man. First name...she paused for a moment to wonder what name she should use. She didn't want to use Sevan; no, she hated Sevan. Brooke. She decided to use Brooke. She glanced up over her head and smirked. She always felt like she could see or really feel something watching her whenever she was in this mode.

What am I looking for? Casual dating sounds like the winner. She thought to herself. She was on a mission to find the man in the ad and didn't exactly know why, but she was fueled with anger still and couldn't stop herself. She glanced at the clock and realized that she was 20 minutes late for her class, but not even that could bring her back to normal.

Occupation? She looked around the room wondering what she should put; self-employed.

Income range? She wanted to meet a prestigious man just like her father, so she put $250,000 plus.

Email? She paused. *Now this is getting tricky.* She opened a new tab on the computer and hurried to make a Yahoo account since she already had a Gmail.

Phone number? Damn they want a lot of information, she thought to herself. So, she opened yet another tab and started a Google Voice phone number.

As soon as the number and email were accepted she was taken to a screen that was a survey that asked a lot more questions. She started to back out at that point, but she just couldn't stop herself.

What age are you looking to date? Do you have children? Would you date someone with children? Would you like to have children? What are the biggest turn offs in a partner? What qualities are you looking for in a partner?

Geez! This is a lot of fucking questions! But yet, she couldn't stop herself.

After 45 minutes of completing the survey she wondered how desperate could people be to have gone through all of this just to meet someone. Just to find love. Her account was now complete, and she had completely missed her class. She still wasn't sure what her goal was at this point, but she knew that she needed to meet the man that looked like her father still.

Steve stared at her and didn't know what to say.

"Steve?"

"Yes?" he asked still not blinking. His mind wandered to so many different directions that this story was about to go with her and each thought he feared tremendously. Every time she told him about her head hurting and her soul leaving her body after her situation with Cherry he was afraid of what was about to be said next.

"Say something. You are staring at me like you don't know who I am," she laughed.

"I don't. I'm learning," he reminded her.

She nodded. "Indeed, you are."

"Did your "soul" ever return to your body like it usually does?"

She shook her head. "Strangely enough, it didn't this time. It was like it had a mind of its own."

Steve never broke his stare and barely blinked. For the first time in his career of 10 years, he feared a client.

"What were you trying to accomplish, Sevan? What was the reason you decided to go on a dating site?"

She shrugged, "I told you. The guy reminded me of my

father, so I wanted to see him."

"You had just hung up with your father screaming and throwing your phone into the wall and then suddenly you wanted to find a man that looks like him?" he asked confusingly.

"Are you calling me a liar, Steve?" she asked with a squint to her eyes.

"No, Sevan. I'm just confused as to what led you to want to find someone who reminds you of someone that hurt you so badly. That's all."

She smiled. "Bathroom break?"

Steve nodded. "Sure. And when you come back would you like to tell me if you found the clone of your father you were searching for?"

Sevan turned to face him as she got closer to the door. "Of course, Steve. I am going to tell you everything you want to know." She smiled and walked out of the room.

Steve took a deep sigh, grabbed his handkerchief, and quickly wiped the sweat from his brow. He kept telling himself to end the session as he saw the sun began to set through the window, but just like Sevan he couldn't stop himself. He was like a blood sucking leech that desired more. It was like watching a scary movie that he couldn't tear himself away from no matter how badly it frightened him. She was so alluring with her looks, her sex appeal, and the way she told the story of her life. He wouldn't be content until he knew more.

My First Time

"God, I hate doing clinical's!" Ryan moaned as she rolled out of bed to get ready.

Sevan was already up and dressed to go. She felt anxious today because she was having her first date with a guy she had been chatting with from the dating site.

"Suck it up. A few more weeks and we graduate." Sevan said as she sat on the bed to put on her tennis shoes.

"What's got into you? Usually I'm telling you that!" she laughed, as she sat up on the side of the bed to attempt to read Sevan.

Sevan never made eye contact she just shrugged. "Nothing. I guess you rubbed off on me."

"Yeah, ok." Ryan said, not believing her.

Sevan struggled with school a lot and if it weren't for Ryan pushing her she wouldn't have made it this far. Ryan continued to watch Sevan as she went through her daily OCD cleaning, making sure the that bed was completely made up without a single crease and straightening her shoes and lotions in order on her dresser. It always intrigued Ryan how neat Sevan was. She on the other hand was the complete opposite, but Sevan would always go behind Ryan and clean her mess up because she couldn't handle seeing it so unorganized.

"What's wrong?" Ryan asked.

"Nothing. Are you going to get ready?" She asked as she began to move Ryan out of the way so that she could clean Ryan's side of the room.

Ryan moved out of her way but continued to stare. "Yes, it is. Tell me," She demanded.

"I said NOTHING!" she yelled as she threw the pillow down on Ryan's bed.

Ryan jumped back out of shock. Sevan had never yelled at her before. When Sevan realized what she did she quickly turned to Ryan to apologize.

"I-I'm sorry. I – I don't know where that just came from," she said, as she sat on the edge of Ryan's bed and stared at the floor.

Ryan paused for a minute, then sat next to Sevan. She gently reached to put her left hand on her back and slowly rubbed it.

"Are you nervous about graduation?" she asked.

Sevan went with it. "Yeah. It's coming so fast," she said, lying about what was really bothering her.

"I don't know what you worried about. You have a job at Cleveland General Hospital waiting on you! Your mom made sure you're set! When I leave here I'll be back on my mother's couch looking for a job." Ryan said as she took her hand off of Sevan and placed it in her lap, realzing she had nothing lined up.

Sevan glanced up at Ryan. "Now you know that's not the case. I can have my mom get you a job fast."

Ryan's eyes lit up. "Really?"

"Of course. If it weren't for you I wouldn't have even made it this far. You know how I struggle with school." Sevan said as she put her arm around Ryan.

"Yeah, well we make a great team. If it weren't for you I'd live in filth!" Ryan said laughing.

Sevan cracked a smile. "Come on, let's get ready to get this over with."

"Cool. Get Out comes out today. Wanna go see it later?" Ryan asked as she headed to the bathroom.

"Uh, I can't. I have to go see my mother," Sevan lied.

Ryan came out the bathroom brushing her teeth and shrugged and turned and walked back in the bathroom as Sevan continued to clean.

"You struggled in school a lot?" Steve interrupted, as he jotted that down in his notes.

Sevan quickly turned her head to face him as she continued to lie on her back. She hated being interrupted.

"Why?" she snapped. "Why is that important to you?"

Steve's eye widened as he saw her becoming slightly angry. "I just thought it was interesting. I didn't gather that from you. That's all." He said lying.

He asked because sociopaths often struggled in school and she was beginning to fit the profile the more she shared with him.

Sevan felt like he was lying to her and sat up straight as they had a staring match.

"I'm sorry. I didn't mean to interrupt. Please, continue." He felt himself beginning to sweat, hoping he didn't upset her to where she wouldn't tell him anymore.

Sevan didn't move right away. She continued to stare at him for a few more minutes as she began to feel their time was running short. The sun began to set, and night was near. She lay back down because she wanted to tell him her complete story before she left.

Ryan decided to go to the movie that night without Sevan. She never minded catching movies alone. She was the only child her parents had so she was used to doing things alone. Sevan was glad that Ryan left before she did because she didn't want her to see her get dressed.

Sevan packed her favorite Victoria Secret bag and headed to meet Kyle, her online love match.

Kyle was one of the men she chose to start a chat with because he looked her father. He was 32 years old and owned his own dental office. From his conversation he seemed like he was genuinely looking for love. Sevan wasn't sure what she was trying to accomplish by meeting with him, but she was going.

She had Uber drop her off at Hyde Park Prime Steakhouse in West Lake; far enough away from her school where no one would notice her. She decided to wear a black mini fitted dress she got from Guess months back. It fit her body perfectly and topped the dress off with a pair of Jimmy Choo pumps and a small black clutch from Aldo. She wore her hair curly and added a dab of MAC lip glass.

When she walked in the restaurant he was already there waiting. He had a table facing the door, so he could see her as she walked in. His posture was perfect as they locked eyes and he paused mid-way drinking his glass of water. His eyes widened because her pictures did her no justice. Her beauty was unmeasurable, and he felt like oxygen left him as she walked closer.

He stood up immediately as she reached the table.

"Brooke?" he asked, to be sure it was her because she was much more beautiful in person than in her pictures.

She smiled. "Yes."

"My apologies, I wanted to be sure it was you. You are absolutely stunning in person," he sincerely said as he walked around the table to pull out her chair.

She sat down feeling a little anxious. "What? Am I ugly

on camera?" she giggled.

He took a deep breath and sat down as anxiety began to arise in him.

"What? No, of course not!"

There was an immediate silence as they both attempted to relax.

"Forgive me for staring, I just can't believe how gorgeous you are," Kyle said nervously.

Sevan giggled. "Thank you."

"Nervous?"

She shook her head. "You?"

He laughed a nervous laugh. "Actually, yes. To be honest, this is my first blind date and you're the first woman I've connected with online. I actually just started my profile."

Sevan's eyebrows raised. "Really?"

He nodded as he sipped his water. "The dating scene was so hard, so I decided to take a chance and see what the online world had to offer. I never expected you, though," he said, blushing.

Sevan couldn't break from looking into his eyes. She could see her father in his features, but not in his eyes; his eyes were kind. They appeared genuine.

"What?" he asked, noticing her staring.

She smiled. "Nothing. I was just looking into your eyes."

"Are they ugly?" he asked jokingly.

"What? No of course not!" she laughed. "They say eyes are the windows to the soul. I like to see if I can tell if you have a good soul or not. It's weird. Forget it," she said waving her hand and setting her napkin in her lap.

"No, no it's interesting. Tell me more," he asked as he reached his hand across the table to relax her.

"I don't know. I just think if I can look into someone's eyes and past the mask they wear I can see what their true intentions are."

He nodded. "Interesting. I've never thought about that. So, what do you see when you look into my eyes?"

She smiled as she gazed into them some more. "I see sincerity."

He smiled. "So, did you tell anyone about our date?"

She shook her head. "Did you?"

"Oh no! I didn't even tell anyone I have a dating profile!" he laughed. "I felt kind of desperate even making one."

Sevan noticed he kept his left hand in his lap, but could see he was moving his hand. "Uh, what are you doing with your left hand?" she asked, frowning her face.

"Hmm?" he stopped movement. "Is it that obvious?" his

face began to turn red.

She turned her head to the left slightly as she still had a confused look on her face, hoping he wasn't at the table masturbating.

"Uh, maybe I should go." She said as she began to get up.

"Wait- wait...no, please." Kyle said as he stood up to reach for her. He pulled his left hand up so she could see it. "Look, it's just a rock."

Sevan paused as she sat back down slowly. "A what?" she asked confusingly.

"A rock." He opened his hand to show her a palm sized colorful rock. The rock was smooth and very beautiful with many colors, mostly different shades of blue in them.

"Why do you have a rock and what are you doing with it?"

He dropped his head in embarrassment. "I'm really shy. Extremely shy. Growing up I would be teased a lot and I was always nervous about meeting people or speaking in front of people. Well I'm the youngest boy of my parents and my older brother, who is the complete opposite of me, traveled for a year straight. I really missed him because I wanted to be like him. I could never travel the world or just climb mountains like he did. He is just so out going. Anyway, he came home at the end of the year and told me he found this rock when he was mountain climbing. He said there was no other rock like it anywhere in sight and he was shocked he even noticed it. He said when he saw it I immediately popped in his head. He said there is no one like me and no matter where I am I stand out. He told me to keep the rock on me and it will calm me whenever I feel nervous just pull it out and hold it."

Sevan smiled. "Really?"

He nodded. "I know it sounds stupid."

"No, it's actually pretty sweet."

"Well, the rock usually works. Usually it calms me down. Today, around you, it's failing me." He laughed.

Sevan took her hand and reached over and put her hand on top of his and he stopped shaking. "Maybe it just needed my touch."

Kyle stared in her eyes feeling like he could really have something with this woman. "Should we go ahead and order?"

Sevan nodded as Kyle called the waitress over. Dinner was nice. The more Kyle opened up, the more relaxed he became, and he finally slid his rock back in his pocket. As they exited the steak house Kyle walked her to the front of the building.

"Where did you park?" he asked, as he looked around.

"I actually took an Uber."

"Uber?"

"Yeah, it's like a taxi service, but not." She laughed. She

felt at ease from the wine.

"Well I can take you where you want to go." He offered.

She took her overnight bag and put it up on her shoulder. "Well I thought if tonight went well I would end it with you."

She caught Kyle off guard when she said that. "Uh, ok. So, what do we do? I don't mean to be square, but I've never done this."

Sevan straightened up. She didn't want to come across as a street walker. "I haven't either. I just thought..." she stopped.

Kyle immediately felt bad about what he said. "No, you're fine," he said, putting his hands on her shoulders and forcing her to gaze up into his eyes.

Sevan looked up at him and even though he was trying to relax her she was beginning to resent him. She didn't know why; she just was.

"I don't want to leave you yet either, this night has been one of the best nights I've had in a long time." He assured her.

Sevan looked up at him. "Really?"

He nodded. "We can talk all night if you like."

"I would like that. Can we get a room?" she asked.

"A room? I have a condo. You can come there. I trust

you," he laughed.

"I've just never been to a hotel and wanted to see what it was like." She lied.

"Oh, well okay. Sure. Hilton okay?"

She nodded.

He extended his left elbow for her to lock her arm around his as he escorted her to his car. He drove a black BMW. Cars and materialistic things didn't impress Sevan because she was raised in money. What impressed her was the thoughtfulness he extended to her and how polite he was. Even though he looked very much like her father his mannerism was different; he wasn't even a charmer and didn't appear to be narcissistic like her father.

When they arrived at the Hilton he valeted the car. He seemed very nervous when they got their room. She was beginning to believe him when he said that he had never done this before. Sevan was beginning to feel slightly uncomfortable, so she avoided eye contact with people or allowed anyone to really notice she was with Kyle. She overheard the receptionist tell him what room they were in, so she walked ahead of him to the elevator.

When he caught up with her it was just the two of them waiting.

"Hey?" He moved closer to her. "You okay?"

She nodded as she stared at the floor. She felt the wine

wearing off and began to ask herself what she was even doing there.

"I ordered us a bottle of the wine you were drinking at the restaurant; I wasn't sure if you wanted more or not." He said trying to make small talk.

He wasn't sure why she began to shut down on him or why she suddenly became quiet and less affectionate. When they stepped off the elevator she walked directly to their room; still ahead of him.

"Brooke, we don't have to do this." He assured her.

She didn't respond or look his way.

"Brooke?" Kyle called her name again.

Forgetting she used an alias she finally looked up at him. "Hmm? No …no I'm fine…this is fine."

Kyle paused before opening the door. "Are you sure?"

"Yes. I just…. I just have never done this either, so I froze up."

Kyle smiled as he stared into her eyes. He believed her and at that moment he was even more intrigued to learn that she was just as nervous as he was. He opened the door and let her go in first.

When Sevan walked in she loved how simple the room was, but the scenery was amazing. She immediately dropped her bag on the couch as she walked straight to the window. The view from where she was at made Cleveland look so beautiful.

Sevan took a deep breath because she felt free at that moment gazing at the night and far away from reality.

"It's beautiful, isn't it?" Kyle said as he came and stood on her left side and stared out the window with her.

"Yes."

"Brooke, we don't have to do anything. I just enjoy your company. We can just sit here and talk until our eyelids can't stay open any longer."

"I'd like that."

At that moment, there was a knock on the door.

"The wine is here."

Sevan smiled as she walked toward the bathroom so that she wouldn't be seen by anyone. Kyle grabbed the wine and tipped the room service and closed the door. Sevan sat on the bed and crossed her legs and slipped a pillow onto her lap because her dress was so short.

As she watched Kyle pour them a glass and slip off his shoes and suit jacket and join her she suddenly felt an uneasy feeling in the pit of her stomach.

"Kyle?"

He handed her a glass of wine and took a sip of his before responding. "Yes?"

"You are perfectly fine with just talking all night?"

He nodded. "Yes."

Sevan wanted to believe him. He appeared sincere. It felt sincere; but staring at him all she could see was her father. The more the wine began to settle the more she felt hatred arise inside her.

"Tell me about your family." Kyle demanded, as he sipped his wine and lay on his left side at the head of the bed to face her.

"What do you want to know?"

"I don't know. Tell me about your mom. What's she like?"

Sevan smiled. "She's beautiful."

"I gather that from looking at you," he said smiling. "What does she do for a living?"

"She's a personal trainer." She lied.

"That's cool. What about your dad?"

"He died."

"Oh, I'm really sorry to hear that."

"It's okay. He wasn't a nice guy anyway," she coldly said as she stared him in the eyes and guzzled the glass of wine quickly. "I don't want to talk about him anymore."

Kyle nodded.

"What about your dad?"

"Oh, my dad is cool. He's going to love you."

"Is he?" she asked, as she raised her brow.

"Yes." He assured her.

"So, you plan to take me home to the family, huh?"

"Is that okay? I would love to see you again."

"How often?"

"Everyday."

Kyle sounded so sure about what he was saying to her. Sevan assumed it was just the wine talking because even though he was sweet she had no intentions on ever seeing him again.

"We'll see," she said, as she handed him her glass of wine.

"More?"

"No. I just want to lay down. My head feels kind of funny."

Kyle immediately moved out of the way as he took her glass and placed it on the night stand next to him. Sevan moved up into the space he freed for her and curled into the fetal position next to him. She closed her eyes and fell right to sleep within seconds.

About 3 am she awoke like she did every night like clockwork, since being raped by her father. Jonathan always found himself in her room at the same time every night he decided to violate Sevan; so, her body had its own alarm clock that never allowed her to sleep at 3am.

When she awoke this time, she had a small panic attack because she forgot where she was, and she could only see Kyle's face because of the moonlight. He was sleeping next to her peacefully fully dressed. He didn't even hear her wake up. Even in his sleep he looked like her father.

Sevan stared at him coldly as she began to replay times Jonathan would have sex with her no matter how much she begged him through tears to stop. He would always tell her if she woke her mother up with the noise he would kill her. Sevan felt anger begin to rise inside of her as tears slowly streamed her face; but never taking her eyes off of Kyle.

The longer she stared the angrier she became; the angrier she became the more her head started to hurt, and she suddenly felt that pop in her head. She looked up over her head and saw her soul floating over her like it always did. This time she stared at it for a while. She felt like it was talking to her. Like it was instructing her to kill Kyle.

She shook her head no as she wiped her tears and continued to stare. Kyle never moved. He was sleeping so peacefully and so comfortably.

Sevan broke the stare from her soul and returned it to Kyle. This time she didn't see Kyle at all. She saw Jonathan. She blinked her eyes a few times and tried to have a clear look, but it was Jonathan. She glanced around the room and she was no longer in the hotel room, she was back in her bedroom, where Jonathan held the power.

She shook her head and closed her eyes as she grabbed her head with both hands. "No! No! No!" she whispered to herself through tears. "Not again!"

She immediately grabbed the pillow she was laying on and put it over Kyle's face and began to press down. At first Kyle didn't move, but once he felt his oxygen getting shorter he tried to fight her off of him. The more he fought the stronger Sevan became as she quickly straddled him to gain more control. She could hear him screaming trough the pillow. Not knowing what was going on he began to panic as he slowly suffocated and died.

Sevan held the pillow still on his face to be sure he wasn't moving any longer as she looked up at her soul over her. She held both hands steady while she continued to straddle him and closed her eyes. She inhaled as she felt her soul reenter her body and the room became the hotel room again and she smiled because Jonathan was finally dead. She slowly removed the pillow and it wasn't Jonathan that was dead; it was Kyle.

Her eyes widened, and she quickly jumped off him as she moved away from the bed backwards and tripped over the table. She scooted backward toward the wall as she stared at the bed and pulled her knees to her chest and began to rock back and forth over and over as tears streamed down her face.

After sitting there of a few minutes in disbelief for what she had just done, she quickly jumped up to clean any evidence of her being in the room. She hurried, but made sure she was thorough. She grabbed her bag and walked over to Kyle's lifeless body and stared at him.

He didn't look dead, he looked as if he were sleeping peacefully. A single tear streamed down her face as she looked down and noticed his right hand holding the rock still. She figured he was nervous just lying there with her; why else would he still be holding it?

Sevan slowly reached in and took the rock from his hand and gripped it as she threw her bag on her left shoulder and walked to the door. She paused as she looked back over her shoulder.

"I'm sorry, Kyle," she whispered to him as she quickly exited the room.

"I don't know why I did that to him." Sevan said as she sat up and reached for a tissue.

Steve didn't move. He felt his heart stop in his chest as he tried to replay what she just said in his mind. He heard of patients confessing murders to their shrinks before, but he had never experienced it until now. He wasn't prepared for that at all. He felt his underarms begin to perspire and hoped his forehead didn't show signs of sweat.

Sevan wiped her face and she became cold in the face again as she directed her attention back to Steve.

"Did I frighten you, Steve?" she said with a half-smile on her face. "I frighten myself at times."

"How…how did you get away without anyone seeing you? When did they find him?"

She chuckled. "I don't know Steve…maybe it was GOD!"

He felt her mocking him and as much as he wanted to reply he didn't because he was unaware of what she could possibly do to him.

"I don't think God helped you escape murder, Sevan."

"No…no maybe not. But He sure as hell didn't stop me, now did He, Steve? She said, challenging him.

"Sometimes He allows things to happen-"

"Happen for a reason…blah blah blah Steve. Ya, know I am so SICK of hearing that bull shit, Steve!" she said, her voice rising.

"What reason did GOD have to let my own FATHER rape me for YEARS? Huh Steve?" she yelled as she jumped up and walked near the window as she paced the floor.

As soon as she jumped up Steve pushed his back into the back of his seat in fear of what she was going to do next.

"And poor Kyle…. what reason did GOD have to let Kyle die?" She turned to face Steve as she snapped at him.

"But…but YOU killed Kyle, Sevan. Not God."

"And did He stop me?" she smirked.

Steve didn't respond.

"But this GOD you love, guess He doesn't love me and He didn't love Kyle."

Sevan folded her arms as she stared at Steve waiting for a response. The room became quiet and the sweat that was on Steve's head couldn't wait any longer as it began to roll down the side of his temples. Sevan saw it and enjoyed knowing she had total control of their session right now.

"I remember when the news reported finding Kyle how they couldn't figure out who would do something to someone as kind and awesome as he was." she said, as she stared at the floor without blinking.

Steve couldn't tell if she felt any remorse or if she enjoyed it. "How did it make you feel to see that on the news?"

Sevan broke out of her trance she was in and looked at Steve. "I felt fine. Sad that it was Kyle, but he must have done something to deserve it. Karma."

Steve gulped hard. She was going to justify her actions in any way she could. She was completely disconnected from feelings.

"Can I tell you some more?"

"I think we may have had enough for today." Steve said.

"Oh great! Because I have so much more to share with you!" she said, ignoring his words as she excitedly plopped down back down on the couch.

Steve wanted to repeat himself, but he was afraid. He had never felt the feeling of fear until that very moment.

"Let me tell you about Greg. Greg looked the most like Jonathan, more than any of them!"

"Them? As in there are more?" Steve swallowed hard.

She smiled.

Ivy Lee

A Gentleman?

"Ryan!" Sevan yelled.

Somehow, even after college, they became roommates and coworkers. Gianni talked them into getting an apartment together so that Sevan didn't have to move back home. She wanted to keep her as far away from Jonathan as she could.

She even cosigned for them to have their first place and helped Ryan get into the Cleveland General Hospital, too. The guilt that she carried about Sevan made her feel like she owed her.

"Ryan! You are so nasty! Why can't you use your own damn bathroom!" Sevan was irritated cleaning up her razors and hair out of the sink.

Ryan came dragging into the bathroom behind her in her tank and panties with her hair tied in a scarf. "Oh, my gawd! Sevan, I'm tired! I'll clean it up later!"

"You wouldn't have to clean it if you used your own damn bathroom!"

"Well, yours has better lighting than mine."

"Yours would have good lighting if you would stop being so lazy and replace the damn bulbs! It's a vanity Ryan! It has multiple lights. When one blows, get another!" she snapped, as she slammed Ryan's razors, alcohol and shaving cream in her arms.

Ryan looked puzzled. "Oh, that's what it is?"

Sevan rolled her eyes and pushed passed Ryan, who followed.

"Vaughn, I'm sorry, okay?" she said sincerely.

"Whatever, Ryan."

"Sevan, really, I am. I'll try and do better."

"Okay." She said as she made sure her make-up was smooth and evenly laid.

"Where you goin'?"

"Out." She said with an attitude still.

"You been going out a lot lately. You got a secret boyfriend?"

Sevan paused as she slowly moved the makeup sponge from her face but stared in the mirror as she could see Ryan staring at her reflection from behind her.

"What would make you think that?"

"I mean you keep getting these little cocktail dresses and your make up is flawless every time and you leave at night. Wait a minute...are you an escort?" she asked with her eyes widened.

Sevan giggled. "No."

"So, you do have a man! Why didn't you tell me? What's his name? What does he look like? He cute? Tall? Good job?"

Sevan turned to face her. "No, I don't have a man."

"Oh." She said disappointedly. "So why you keep dressing up and leaving?"

Sevan couldn't think of a lie. "Because." She rolled her eyes. "Because I'm hoping to maybe meet one."

Ryan smiled. "Well why didn't you say something? I'll get dressed and we can go have drinks and meet guys!"

Sevan quickly stopped her and put her right hand up. "No, no that's okay. I want to go alone."

Ryan's smile disappeared. "Okay."

"It's not like that Ry, I swear. It's just easier for me to meet and brush them off when I don't like them." She said as he glanced at her watch.
"I gotta go though. I'm late."

"Late to meet random guys, huh?" Ryan said rolling her eyes as she walked out of the room.

Sevan wanted to stop her, but changed her mind because she didn't want to keep Greg waiting.

Greg was another match that she had been talking too for the last five months since Kyle. She wanted to shut down her profile, but she couldn't. The feeling and the rush that she got after killing Kyle...she desired it again. She tried to fight it and hoped that it would go away, but the desire grew stronger, and stronger and the more that she talked to Greg the more she felt like she needed to fulfill her desire.

If Greg didn't look exactly like Jonathan she may have been able to walk away easier, but right before she was going to shut down her profile he messaged her. It had to be fate, right?

Sevan hopped in her Uber, and this time she wasn't nervous at all. She was excited to see her next victim...date.

"You a real pretty girl, how old are you?" the elderly Uber lady- driver asked, attempting to make conversation.

Sevan was leaning forward as she stared out the window. She heard the woman, but it didn't register what she was saying because she was so focused on what she was going to do when she met Greg.

"Hmm? Oh, thank you." She said as she glanced at the woman then immediately back out the window.

"How old are you?" she asked again.

"Um, 27," she lied.

"Well, you are really young looking. That's a blessing."

Sevan rolled her eyes. Anything that even remotely sounded like God to her made her sick to her stomach.

"Excited about your date?"

"What?" Sevan gave the woman her undivided attention. "Who said I had a date?"

She became paranoid.

"Well, yah all dressed up and yah won't sit back in the seat. I figured you were meeting a man. Maybe even a first date." The older woman said smiling.

Sevan quickly sat back. She didn't like that the lady was reading her the way she was, and it made her nervous.

"I remember first dates." She began reminiscing about her younger days. "The anxiety of being with your crush for the first time. The first laugh. The first hug. The first kiss. The scent of the cologne."

"Okay, I get it, but this is not that," she reassured her.

The elderly lady laughed. "Okay. Whatever you say, but chile' you didn't put that fancy dress and make up on for nothing."

Sevan folded her arms across her chest as if she was covering up the look of being dressed for a date. The elderly lady smiled as she looked in the mirror at her.

"Well, yah look simply gorgeous," she said, hoping to ease how she just made Sevan feel.

Sevan smiled a half smile and relaxed her hands in her lap. "Thanks."

"Hmmm-mmm. Now, make sure he treats you as beautiful as you look," she said, as she parked the car and turned to look her in the eyes. "Have fun, chile'," she said with a grandmotherly smile.

Sevan wanted to avoid eye contact with her, but she couldn't. She paused before getting out of the car and had an uneasy feeling about it all.

"Would you like me to come back to get you chile' jus' in case?" the woman said reading her nervousness.

Sevan quickly dismissed it. "No, no, I'm fine thank you." She said as she tried to exit the car quickly.

The elderly woman watched her walk into Hotel Indigo as she smiled and shook her head. "Weird girl." She said to herself as she pulled off.

Sevan paused to fix her clothes before she walked into the restaurant of the hotel. She looked in the mirror on the wall as she made sure her lipstick and hair were still intact.

Brooke...you are BROOKE tonight, she reminded herself silently before she walked in.

Just as Kyle had waited for her, so did Greg. Greg was the spitting image of her father, and she almost lost it the closer she got to him, the more that she could see that he looked just like Jonathan.

"Brooke?" he said, smiling as he stood up.

Sevan smiled. "That would be me."

Greg walked around the table quickly as he pulled her chair out for her.

"Ah, a gentleman, are you?" she said as she sat down and allowed him to scoot her chair up for her.

As he walked back to his side of the table and sat down her chuckled. "Not really. I just wanted to make a good impression. Did it work?" he smiled.

"A wise guy, too, huh?" she said, smiling.

He laughed. "I'm teasing. You look beautiful, by the way."

Sevan paused as she gazed into his eyes. He was much younger than her father was, but unlike Kyle she could see Jonathan in his eyes. She could see the ill intentions; the deep hidden secrets he possessed. She felt like she was staring at pure evil. She felt comfortable about what she was about to do to Jonathan...Greg.

Greg was dressed in a gray suit with a white button-down dress shirt, but left the top button off. He was dressed more like business casual; same way Jonathan dressed. He had a very arrogant demeanor about himself and the more she analyzed it the more at ease she was about killing him.

She immediately relaxed and gave a soft smile as she stared in his eyes. Greg assumed she was flirting, but all she could picture was him suffocating and begging for air as she held the pillow over his face.

"So, what made you choose this place?" Sevan asked as

she looked around and then back into his eyes.

Greg smirked as he picked up the glass of whisky sour he'd ordered before she got there, resting his right elbow on the table as he lifted the glass to his lips, making sure he never released the eye contact he had with her. Now he was flirting and hoped that she picked up on it and flirted back.

Sevan definitely picked up on it because it was the same looks Jonathan would sneak and give her at the dinner table when her mother wasn't looking. Her stomach turned as she remembered those moments.

"I take it you've done this often?" she assumed, as she crossed her arms and leaned her back deeper against the chair.

Greg took another sip of his liquor and placed it back on the table.

"Why don't you order yourself a drink?" He suggested, in hopes that it would loosen her up.

"I think I will. What are you drinking?" she asked.

"Whisky sour. Straight." He smiled as he continued to stare.

"I'll have one too…. double please."

Greg kept locking eyes with her as he waved his left hand to signal for the waitress to come over. She immediately walked over. She was a bit jealous to see Sevan sitting with him since he had been flirting with her while he waited for Sevan to get there.

"Yes, Sir?" she said, staring at him and pretending Sevan wasn't sitting there, as he pretended the waitress wasn't standing there because his gaze was still on Sevan.

"Can you bring me another one, please? And a double for her?"

"Yes, Sir," she said as she finally allowed her eyes to see what he was so intrigued by.

Sevan was definitely intriguing, and the waitress to catch herself as she was mesmerized by her beauty too.

Sevan could feel the two of them falling into a trance over her as she kept a side smirk and arms softly folded across her chest. She slowly turned her head to lock eyes with the waitress.

Sevan had no interest in women at all, but she locked eyes with her the same way she did with Greg and made her feel slightly intimidated.

"Uh...uh.. did you want that on the rocks?" she stuttered a little.

It was like Sevan was doing voodoo with her eyes on them.

"Straight up... just like his," she said seductively.

"Yes, of course," she said as she hurried away from the table.

Sevan returned her attention to Greg. "So, do you do this

often?"

Greg smiled. "I enjoy life, if that's what you mean."

"Is this where you come to enjoy life often?" she wouldn't let up.

Greg laughed. "Why ask questions you don't want to really know the truth about? Why not just enjoy our time together? No woman really wants to hear about another woman. All you will do is over analyze anything I tell you. Probably obsess about it; compete with her in your head and try your best to outdo her to keep my attention on you all the while driving yourself completely insane and you wouldn't even know if I were telling you the truth about other women or just fucking with your mind so that I can keep you under my thumb the whole time."

Silence fell at the table as Sevan took in what he just said. They both stared at each other and simultaneously reached for their drink and took deep sips this time.

He was definitely a younger version of her father. As much as she hated Jonathan she was still intrigued by his demeanor and Greg was exactly like him.

Sevan took her drink and finished it off as Greg raised his eyebrow.

"Would you like another?" he said, as he finished his to keep up with her.

"No. I'd like to go to the room," she said, smiling. Her liquor hit her fast and she felt sexy and confident.

"I thought you'd never ask," he said as he pulled his room key out.

She knew he most likely had a room; probably his favorite room that he took every woman to.

"Noooo," she moaned seductively which quickly got his attention. "Not here."

Greg looked confused. "I already booked the room."

"I'm sure you did. You made enough memories here. Let's go somewhere else," she said as she slid her right leg toward him and gently rubbed it against his.

"But it's paid for," he said as he became frustrated.

"So? Pay for another one." She said sternly as she sat up straight and looked him directly in his eyes as if to tell him this wasn't up for negotiation.

Greg was intrigued by her sternness and decided a woman this confident can have whatever she wanted. She wasn't like his usual hook ups; no she was far more unusual. She was someone he could see his self with a lot longer than a fling for the night.

Greg left the money with more than enough to cover the tip on the table as he stood up and slowly buttoned his suit jacket so that Sevan could see his erection; exactly how her father would do. Her eyes immediately went to it then back to him as he was buttoning his jacket, smirking.

Sevan returned the smirk as she finally fully convinced herself that the world would be a better place without another Jonathan.

Sevan stood up slowly as she kept the gaze locked into his eyes and reached her left hand out to him as he extended his right hand to take hers and guided her around the table and closer to him.

The waitress watched them from the bar with envy as she never blinking. She had Greg's attention before Sevan arrived, but nothing like she had right now. She watched Sevan walk seductively in her heels; it was like watching a model.

She continued to watch them until they were no longer visible, out of the door. She never blinked until they were gone and when she did a tear fell from her left eye. She quickly wiped it and looked around to see if anyone noticed and hurried back to work.

As they got outside to the parking lot Sevan looked to the sky as she usually does and looked for the moon. It wasn't visible; it peaked through the clouds and she got an eerie feeling about the rest of the evening instantly.

She shook it off as she was stopped at a silver Lexus. Greg couldn't take his eyes off of her. Sevan stood there as the uneasy feeling began to subside in her stomach. She figured it may have just been the liquor.

Greg opened the door for her and she slowly got in. he quickly closed the door and hurried to the driver side. Sevan didn't feel the feeling in her head like she usually does. She felt completely normal. She continued to look to the sky for the moon and it was like it was playing a game of hide and seek with her right now. She felt herself getting angry inside.

"Did you have a hotel in mind you wanted to go to?" he asked, as he drove up the strip passing many different hotels in the Beachwood area.

At this point it could have been a hole in the wall for all he cared. He just wanted to be inside of her right now. Sevan focused on finding the moon; she never heard a word Greg said.

"Brooke?"

"Hmmm?" she said, still looking to the sky.

"What are you looking at?" he asked, in a frustrated manner.

"What?" she said, not paying him any attention.

The clouds had completely covered the moon and she became angry and furious inside. She needed the moon. It always channeled her soul for her and right now she was all alone.

"I don't care," she snapped, as she folded her arms. "Just not where you been before with anyone else."

Greg turned his head toward her immediately as he noticed a shift in her attitude and posture. His erection went down as he felt like he was in a relationship with this woman versus a fun date.

Sevan realized the vibe she gave off from the way he turned his head to face her. It was the same way Jonathan looked at her after they left the movies when she was a teen. She quickly snapped back into character and unbuckled her seat belt.

She slid her body on her knees in the seat as she turned toward him and leaned over and slowly took her right hand and slid it on his thigh and she kissed his ear lobe slowly.

She softly moaned in his ear as she eased her hand on his penis and felt his erection immediately come back. She knew what he liked; he was Jonathan. She knew exactly what he liked.

Greg moaned as she caressed him, and he forgot that she just snapped at him. Her touches were gentle, and she knew exactly how to touch him. She was definitely experienced even though all her emails between them said different. He didn't care; he wasn't going to marry her, anyway. He didn't even plan on seeing or calling her again after tonight.

Sevan could tell he was quickly forgetting how she just treated him and was falling back into the moment.

She gently unbuckled his pants and slid her hand inside his pants as she kissed his ear lobe softly. Greg let out a deeper moan.

"Find us a hotel," she whispered in his ear.

Greg was becoming impatient and wanted to have sex with her now. He really didn't want to pay for another room since he had already paid for his other hotel.

He drove around the Beachwood area looking for a hotel and as he drove he saw a construction for Cleveland General Hospital and decided to turn into it.

Sevan slowly slid back away from him as she looked around.

"Where are you going?" she asked nervously.

"I want you now. I can't wait," he said, as he parked his car quickly behind the dumpster and shut the lights off before passing cars noticed him.

"No...you said we were getting a room," Sevan said.

Greg ignored her as he ripped his belt off his pants and threw it on her side of the car. He pulled his pants completely down as he pushed his seat back. He was drunk, and his romantic side completely disappeared as he became more barbaric.

Sevan's heart rate picked up because she didn't plan for this. She thought she would be able to pull the good girl act like she did with Tyler and smother him quickly.

Greg was nothing like Tyler. He was aggressive, and she felt that he may even rape her. She froze up as she didn't know how she would be able to suffocate him without the pillow. Her only advantage to be able to kill is to be on top. She looked through the sunroof begging the moon to come out. She knew if the moon were there she would be unstoppable…. but just like God, it never came.

Greg reached over and grabbed her aggressively and pulled her on top of him and began to kiss her. Before Sevan could fight him off she went with the flow because he was much stronger than she was right now.

Her black dress rose up her thighs as he forced them to straddle him. She felt his member become harder as it touched the outside of her panties and pressed against her vagina.

He pulled her closer to force her to grind on him as he sat up and began to kiss her neck softly. Her body had a natural reaction to the feeling, but inside she was panicking like when Jonathan snuck in her room at night.

She closed her eyes and hated her body for enjoying his touches. She blamed the alcohol and denied the physical attraction to Greg. He began to moan as he kissed all of her neck and slid her breast from the top of her dress.

Sevan kept her eyes closed as she began to relax and let him kiss on her. She naturally began to grind her clitoris on his erect member as she slid her arms around his neck and held on. She was falling deeper into the moment as she returned his kiss and slowly dropped her head so that her lips met his. She didn't see the look alike of Jonathan anymore; this time it was Jonathan.

Her heart rate picked up and as she got scared and the car became her bedroom when she was 16 again. Greg never noticed her energy switch and continued to kiss on her nipples. Like always, her body enjoyed it, but the kid inside of her was screaming.

She closed her eyes and titled her head back as she kept saying to herself *NO NO NO NO NO NO NO!*

She was unaware that she had begun to say it aloud until she heard Greg whisper to her in between kisses *YES, YES, YES...*

At that moment she felt the pop in her head and she opened her eyes. She watched the clouds move to only reveal the moon, which she was eagerly waiting on. Her sly grin began to surface as they picked up the pace, as Sevan grind on Greg. She knew the moon wouldn't fail her as this false god did her entire life. Her soul began to watch her like it always did as she took a sigh of relief and felt empowered.

Sevan grinned as she sat up straight and gave Greg eye contact. She continued to grind on him as she felt her thong become moist.

Greg moaned. "I can feel you."

Sevan smiled as she leaned in and began to kiss his neck and slowly lick it while he relaxed and closed his eyes. She continued to grind on him as she looked to her left and noticed the belt on her side of the car. She took her left hand and slowly grabbed it.

Greg opened his eyes to see what she was doing as she slid it around his neck and held on to the straps with both hands as she sat straight up and began to grind in a circular motion on his member.

"Ooohhh, kinky, are you?" he moaned in excitement.

She kept her grin as she began to slowly buckle the belt together and slowly pull the strap to where it was fitted around his neck but not too tight.

Greg was enjoying the moment and he didn't realize that he liked the bondage until she did it. Normally he wouldn't trust it, but there was something about Sevan that took him in and deep under her spell.

Sevan could see in his eyes that he was enjoying everything she was doing so she picked up her pace grinding on him as she slowly began to tighten the belt strap. Greg moaned in ecstasy as they locked eyes.

"Do you like it baby?" she whispered.

"Mmmm-hmmm," he moaned.

"Say you like it." she whispered.

"I like it," he moaned.

"Say you like it!" she demanded, as she tightened the belt and picked up her pace some more.

"I like it!" he moaned louder, as he took his right hand to adjust the grip of the belt.

Sevan quickly smacked his hand down.

"It's..too..tight," he said as he tried to keep his normal breathing.

Sevan smiled as she took her left hand and slid her panties to the side to distract him as she allowed his member to feel the

warmth of her vagina. Greg closed his eyes as their flesh touched each other and moaned.

"Brooke...Mmmm," He moaned.

Sevan knew she had him then and she quickly tightened the belt and his body jerked.

"What..the...fuck!" he gasped trying to get some air.

Sevan's grin deepened as she pulled tighter. Greg's face became bright red, and on human instinct instead of pushing her off of him he reached for the belt and tried to loosen it with both hands. She instantly squeezed tighter.

She gripped her thighs around him to keep herself grounded as he struggled to free himself and she climaxed on top of him as she squeezed. The rush from watching him gasp for air turned her on. As she felt her legs shake she tightened them on him and squeezed harder.

Greg's eyes locked with hers as he started to lose consciousness. He released his right hand and unexpectedly he punched her in the jaw. Sevan's head hit the window, but she held her grip. Greg was a fighter. She didn't expect that. She pegged him to be like Tyler from their emails.

They began to tussle in the driver seat. Greg was fighting for his life as he used the left hand to try and be a barrier between his neck and the belt. Sevan tried her hardest to get more strength in her. Her orgasm took some of her energy, but fear that he would kill her before she killed him gave made her adrenalin pump harder.

"Fucking ...bitch!" Greg muffled through breaths.

Sevan never spoke; she just pulled the leather belt as hard as she could. Greg became weak and began to nod out as both his hands dropped. Sevan wasn't sure if he was tricking her, so she kept pulling the belt until he had no life in him. Tyler had the pillow over his face, so she never saw life leaving him as she did up close and personal with Greg. She became excited as she watched his pupils began to dilate. Even working in the hospital, she had never gotten to see anyone die yet.

She felt a rush come over her body as she sat on top of him and let the belt go slowly. She leaned in as she studied his eyes under the moonlight and smiled.

She looked up and her soul began to return to her body again. As she took it in she hopped off him and sat in the passenger seat as she reached for her purse. She grabbed a cloth and alcohol pads out and began to wipe herself down and quickly wiped his penis off. She wanted to ensure none of her DNA was on him.

Sevan quickly reached for her cell phone and turned on the flash light, as she scanned his feet slowly and up his body to make sure that none of her hair fell out from the tussle.

As she reached his face with the light his eyes looked empty as they stared at her. She got closer as she could see that the evil in him was gone. She gave a sinister laugh.

"Didn't see that coming did you, Jonathan?" she yelled, as she followed it with a chuckle mixed with emotions of sadness and anger.

She sat back in the passenger seat and began to get her things together as she adjusted her clothes and continued to ramble on.

"You never expected to me to be so strong, did you Jonathan?" she said, as she rubbed her hand across the floor of the car to make sure she didn't drop anything.

"You thought I would always be weak! That you could just keep touching things that didn't belong to you! DIDN'T YOU!" she yelled, as tears slowly followed.

She paused and looked over at Greg. His eyes and mouth were still wide opened as he faced her.

"Oh, you in shock?" she laughed. "Yeah, well, me too," she said, shrugging as she flipped the mirror down to check her hair.

When her eyes met the mirror she saw the bruise that he left when he'd punched her in the face. She paused and slowly moved her hand to touch it.

"Oh...my...what did you do?" she whispered as she turned her face to get a better look at the bruise left on her jaw.

She continued to rub her face gently.

"You are ALWAYS hurting me! ALWAYS! I fuckin' HATE you!" she screamed at the mirror.

She quickly turned to Greg. "I fucking HATE you Jonathan! I

HATE you! I'm glad you're dead! I hope you rot in the same hell you created for me!" she screamed.

"I fucking HATE you!" Sevan screamed, as she realized she was in the therapist office and not in the car with Greg any longer.

She felt the control she had over the session dying when she realized that she had allowed her emotions to show. She quickly regained her composure when she saw that Steve was just staring at her.

Steve was afraid of her. He didn't want to show it, but he was terrified. He was so terrified that he didn't know how to end the session when he realized the sun was almost gone and the moon would soon take over the sky.

From the details that she shared, he feared that the moon would channel her to kill again.

Silence was between them as he tried to figure out what to say to her next. There was nothing in the text books he studied throughout college to prepare him for this moment and no amount of experience to prepare him for a case like hers. He was stuck, and fear took over his body.

"Steve." Sevan broke the silence.

"Ye- yes?" he said clearing his throat.

"Do you have anything you want to say? I feel like you're judging me right now Steve."

"I would never judge you, Sevan. I'm curious on how you got away? You left with bruises. How could you cover that up? Ryan wasn't the least bit curious when you came home?"

Sevan laughed. "Of course, she was. I just simply ripped my dress, threw a shoe, ruffled my hair and broke the strap on my purse and told her I almost got mugged, but I fought back and escaped."

Steve paused. "She believed you?"

Sevan giggled. "Steve, every woman that cries wolf is believable. It's the ones that really need help that no one believes."

Steve had no response. He began to recall hearing about a man in the news that was found at a Cleveland General Hospital construction site in his car murdered. It aired earlier in the year. He never expected to hear confessions from that man's murderer.

"Were you content then, Sevan? Was your appetite for killing innocent men satisfied after being able to see Greg dead up close and personal?"

Sevan's facial expression changed as she became upset again.

"I didn't kill Greg... I killed Jonathan!"

"No, Sevan, you killed Greg. And you killed Kyle. Jonathan was never there."

Sevan paused as she tried to recollect those days and stared at the floor. She knew she wasn't crazy. She definitely killed Jonathan.

"No...Steve...."

"Sevan, think about it. Jonathan is still alive. You killed Kyle and Greg."

"No...I killed JONATHAN!"

"How Sevan? How can you kill him twice?" he tried to make her realize what she had done.

"Twice? Who said I killed him twice?" she stared in his eyes with her sinister smirk.

"You did. Correct?" he was confused.

She laughed. "Steve, I've killed Jonathan about 10 times so far."

Steve's heart rate picked up. "What? Who else did you kill?"

She shrugged, "Eh, I don't know. A few Jonathans. They were all the same. Date, drinks, hotel, suffocate.... the usual. I just had my favorites. Greg was the only fighter I had though."

"Why suffocation, Sevan? Why did you enjoying suffocating them?"

"That's how I felt every time Jonathan would come into my room. I felt like he was suffocating me." She slowly moved her hands to her neck, like she was choking.

"I felt like he was taking the air from my body and I couldn't

stop him. At times I wished he would just kill me and get it over with. Death was too easy. Dying from it all would've been too easy, don't you think Steve?"

"I don't believe death is the answer."

"So, you think it was ok for him to come in my room whenever he felt like it?" She became angry at Steve immediately.

"No. I believe he should be locked up and punished for what he has done to you. I don't believe Kyle or Greg, or the others you speak of should have paid the price for what he has done to you."

"You believe in God right, Steve?" she said, as she sat back on the couch.

He nodded.

"What about Jesus?"

He nodded again. "Do you?"

"So, tell me, did Jesus deserve to die for all of humanity? He was the most righteous man that walked the earth, correct?" she asked ignoring his question.

Steve nodded. "Yes, he was the most righteous."

"So, we are told…. we are told he did no wrong to anyone, correct? That's what they want us to believe, right?"

He nodded again. She laughed when he nodded.

"So, who the fuck is Kyle? Or Greg? Or any of the others that they are so much better than the most righteous man that ever walked the earth that they couldn't pay for the sins of Jonathan?"

Steve paused. "But the bible says not to murder."

Sevan laughed again. "The bible says a lot of shit, Steve. Not to murder...but they killed Jesus. Oh, please Steve! Do they talk about rape in the bible being a sin too? Or molesting of children?"

"Vengeance is mine says the Lord." Steve threw in. "God will avenge you, Sevan."

"No, Steve. God will not. See, God didn't stop him when he came in my room, no matter how many times I called for this pathetic god. So, I guess He picks and chooses who He avenges, huh?"

Steve had no words. He didn't even want to have any for her. It was against the rules to even discuss religion, but somehow all he knew to speak to her on was God. Nothing from college he could remember to help her at all.... just God.

"I'm sorry for what he did to you, Sevan."

"What are you sorry for?"

"You didn't deserve it. You were innocent."

"I **was** innocent? Was? Not anymore, huh?" she laughed.

"I have a question, Sevan."

"Shoot."

"Have you ever had a relationship outside of the internet dating? Anything in the dating field besides the men you meet that look like Jonathan?"

She smiled as she dropped her head and blushed. Just the thought of Za-Non made her smile.

"Just one. The last eight months. My fiancé. Za-Non."

"Fiancé?" Steve asked as he immediately looked over for her ring. He had never seen her with a ring before and hoped she wasn't delusional about being engaged.

"Yeah," She said, as she smiled and sent her attention toward the window.

"Did you meet him online as well?"

"Oh, no...of course not."

"Does he look like Jonathan too?"

She looked at Steve and her smile disappeared. "Nothing at all like him."

"Can we talk about Za-Non?"

Ivy Lee

Za-Non

"Ry, if you don't stop following me around I'm going to lose my mind!" Sevan yelled, searching the apartment for her favorite work out tennis shoes as Ryan was quick on her heels.

"No! I am most definitely going with you! It's not safe for you to go anywhere by yourself anymore!"

Ryan had been doing everything with Sevan for the past month ever since she came home late one night screaming about someone trying to attack and rob her.

Sevan paused in the living room and turned to face her.

"Ry.... where are my shoes?"

Ryann shrugged. She had borrowed the shoe a few days before and forgot to bring them from her locker at the hospital.

"Ryan?" Sevan said, in a calm but sarcastic tone.

"Yeah?"

"Stop touching my shit!" she yelled, as she walked around her and back to her bedroom to get a different pair out of her closet.

Ryan followed her to her room. "I'm sorry. I'll return them when I get back to work. But I am serious. I don't feel like working out, but I'll just come to the gym.

"For what? That's stupid Ryan!"

"I don't know," she said as she leaned against the wall and folded her arms. "I just couldn't take it if something happened to you. You're like my sister."

Sevan paused from putting on her shoe and looked at Ryan. She never had anyone closer to her than Ryan and she felt emotional when she heard her say that she was like a sister to her.

"Ryan, nothing is going to happen to me. Look how I was able to defend myself and get away! I'll be fine," she assured her.

"Okay, I'll stay home today, but if I don't feel right I'm popping up at that gym. Deal?" she asked.

"Deal," Sevan said, as she finished putting on her shoes. She jumped up and gave Ryan a quick hug and hurried off to the gym at Legacy Village.

Today the gym was much more crowded than usual and it kind of irritated her, so she quickly threw her bag in a locker, threw on her Beats headphones, and turned her music up to the maximum as she searched through Pandora for a rap station.

As she left the women's locker room looking down at her phone she walked right into the cutest guy she'd seen since her 16th birthday party.

He was 6'3", had hazel green eyes, and his hair was straight and to the back with a light beard; he has the bad boy look like Jax on *Sons of Anarchy*.

His tan was beautiful, and she knew that he didn't get it

from the Cleveland weather. He must have traveled somewhere. Sevan was instantly attracted to him. He had his shirt off and his abs looked like you could wash clothes on them.

"Get out of that phone and watch where you're going," he said with a smile.

Sevan didn't hear a word he said. Between his gorgeous mesmerizing smile and her loud music, she was completely distracted.

"What?" she said, knowing that she still couldn't hear him and she immediately pulled one of her earbuds out.

"I said watch where you're going."

"Oh..." Sevan gave a bashful giggle.

Sevan didn't move she just stood there in the same kind of trance that she usually put on others. The beautiful stranger was just as mesmerized as she was. He smiled and walked around her and headed to the men's locker room.

Sevan had hoped that he wasn't done working out and that she would be sure to run into him again. She walked away and put her ear phones back in and headed to the treadmill for a jog.

About 10 minutes into jogging she glanced to her right and there was the stranger jogging right beside her. She had been so focused in her workout she didn't even notice when he got on his treadmill.

Her eyes immediately fell to the sweat that was now dripping over his temples and his chest. It wasn't a heavy sweat; just enough to make his tan sexier.

She began to lose her pace when he looked toward her as he continued his jog and smiled at her. She turned her head forward instantly and tried to regain her focus, but she couldn't so she stopped her machine, jumped off, and walked to the weight area.

The stranger did exactly what she did and followed behind her. Sevan sat on the machine to work out her inner thighs and he sat on the one right next to her.

"I didn't plan on leg day today, but I guess I'll make an exception," he said as he changed the weights to a heavier set.

Sevan's heart beat picked up the pace. She was doing cardio without even working out, just being around him. Her stomach began to do flips as she attempted to pretend that he wasn't there.

She began to fumble with adjusting the weights because she was so nervous. He picked up on it and took it as a sign that she was just as interested as he was, so he got off his machine to help her.

"Here, I got you. How much weight can you handle?" he asked, as he took the pin and waited for her to answer him.

As she sat there and slowly allowed her eyes to meet his she felt her heart beat pick up the pace even more. She felt herself began to sweat.

"It's really hot in here," she said softly, unable to find the words to answer his question.

He chuckled, and his smile made her knees weak. "Would you like me to put it on a lighter set of weights?"

She nodded slowly. "Yes."

He smiled again as he set the pin to 35lbs for her. "Za-Non."

"Hmm?" she asked confusingly.

"My name is Za-Non, but you can call me Z. What's your name?" he asked, as he kneeled on his right knee to get closer to eye level with her as he extended his right hand.

Sevan felt her hands tremble slightly as she extended her hand to meet his. "Hey, Z." she said with a smile.

"Your name?" he asked again as he raised an eyebrow.

"Oh, Sevan," she giggled.

"Sevan, that's pretty. What does it mean?"

"Who said it has a meaning?"

He smiled. "Awe, come on Sevan. Everything in life has a meaning. What's the meaning of your name?"

She smiled as she eased up a little while he still held her hand intentionally.

"It means seven in Arabic."

"Seven? Why seven?"

She laughed. "You sure ask a lot of questions."

"Well, how can you learn anything in life if you don't ask?" he said smiling.

"What exactly are you trying to learn?" she asked, as she attempted to release her hand.

He felt her pulling back and held her hand a little tighter. "Everything."

"Is that so?" she said as they continued their intense eye contact.

"Yes. So, again, why seven?"

Giving in to his request she answered him. "Seven because I was the seventh pregnancy."

"Oh, you are the seventh child? Out of how many?"

"No, I was the seventh and only pregnancy that made it."

"Interesting. Lucky number seven," he said smiling.

As soon as he said that she immediately released the grip he had on her hand because that's what her father always said about her.

"Did I say something wrong?" he asked with genuine concern.

"I don't know how lucky I really am if that's what it means." She sounded kind of down.

"Well, I'm the lucky one today," he said smiling.

"How so?"

"I'm having a conversation with the most beautiful woman in this gym," he said smiling.

She blushed. "Yeah, ok," she said as she turned her head so that he wouldn't see her blushing.

"I would be even luckier if that same beautiful woman would allow me to take her to dinner tonight."

"Tonight?"

"Well, after working out I'm sure you'd like to replenish yourself. I know I sure would. And I'd love it if you would accompany me," he said, as silence fell between them as they gazed at each other.

His eyes were warm and inviting, sort of like Kyle's were. It was rare that she met kind eyes.

"Or we can just stay here and stare at each other all night," he said, smiling to break the silence.

She embarrassingly giggled. "No, we can go to dinner."

"Great. What time can I pick you up?"

"I'll meet you."

"Meet me?"

"Yes."

"No, I want to pick you up so that we can talk on the way there."

"I don't know you. You could be some kind of serial killer."

He laughed. "Serial killer? Do I look like I could harm a fly?" he asked, as he stretched both arms out as if to say *take a good look at me.*

She laughed. "Looks can be deceiving."

He laughed. "Fair enough. But I could never see myself harming someone as precious as you."

She didn't respond. She just stared at him. He was being honest, and she could feel it.

"So, is 8 o'clock a good time?"

She nodded.

"Good," he said as he took her cell phone from her left hand and stored his number in it.

"Call me."

She smiled as she reached for her phone. He began to hand it back to her and then suddenly pulled back. She was confused.

"Better yet, I'll call myself right now, so I can just save your number."

"Oh yeah?" she said, as she raised her eyebrows and smiled.

"Yeah." He said smiling and standing up as he handed her

back her phone after he called himself.

"Just in case you fall asleep and need me to wake you up. This strenuous workout you did today may make you sleepy after you take a shower."

She laughed. "Oh, you got jokes?"

He smiled and shrugged.

"I don't recall you doing much more than I did Mr. Za-non," she giggled.

"Actually, I was already done working out when you bumped into me, but I told myself that I couldn't leave here unless I at least knew your name."

She stopped smiling. "So, you pretended to work out just to know my name?"

He smiled. "I'll see you later."

"How did that make you feel?" Steve asked even though it was apparent on her face that she enjoyed what Za-Non said and did.

She took a deep breath. "I felt like a normal girl."

"How long ago was this?"

"Ten months ago," she said smiling as she recalled it like it was yesterday.

"Ten months? And you're engaged already?" Steve asked.

She nodded. "He said he knew from the minute he saw me that I was his wife."

Steve nodded. "That's possible."

"When he mentioned the serial killer statement did that bother you?" He needed to know.

Sevan's smile quickly disappeared. "Why would that bother me, Steve?"

He paused as to choose his words carefully.

"Well, because you've killed before. I just wondered if it bothered you that he mentioned it."

"Well, no. I'm not a serial killer, Steve. So, no," she said in a serious but irritable manner.

Steve decided to back down and switch subjects.

"Did Za-Non curve the appetite for killing Jonathan? Was it finally over when you met him?"

She laughed, "What does Z have to do with Jonathan?"

"So, you were cheating on Za-Non?" he pursued the conversation.

"Cheating? I would never cheat on him!" she sounded offended.

"Well, every time you log into your dating profile and entertain other men for any purpose other than friendship that could be looked at as a form of cheating," he explained.

Sevan paused as she didn't look at it this way. Steve hoped that him saying that would make her think twice about killing again. He hoped that he could stop her in some way or at least get her to see her wrongs.

She began to cry softly. Steve wasn't sure if the tears were real or not.

"What's the matter?"

"I cheated on Za-Non with Jonathan! How could I do something like that to him?"

Steve couldn't tell if she were faking or genuine because sociopaths often didn't feel remorse and then she suddenly stopped crying and it turned into a wicked laughter.

Steve's heart began to race. Her laugh was eerie, sinister; very wicked. He feared what she may say next.

"Steve, PLEASE!" she yelled as the laughter completely stopped.

"I will kill Jonathan until he no longer exists! Until all of the Jonathans in this world are DEAD I will- not- stop!"

Steve took a hard swallow. "So, is it safe to say you've killed since you've been with Za-Non?"

She smiled.

"Does he ever have a clue as to where you are when you

are killing?"

"He knows where I am."

"He knows that you are murdering innocent people?"

"Innocent? Jonathan isn't innocent!"

"The men you've killed. They were innocent, Sevan," he reminded her.

"Were they really, Steve? Or did they have secret sins just like Jonathan?"

"Sevan, where does Za-Non think you are when you are killing people?" he asked again, but rephrased himself this time.

"He knows where I am, Steve," she repeated.

He was confused.

"Brooke is the one punishing Jonathan. She has to. He hurt Sevan for so long. Since God wouldn't save her, Brooke did."

Steve paused as to take in how she was now referring to Brooke as another person. He didn't write anything on his note pad any longer. He decided he would review the recording later and make notes.

"How many more were there since you met Za-Non?"

She shrugged. "I can only remember my favorites."

"Favorites?"

"There were some that I enjoyed more than others."

"How many favorites did you have since you met Za-Non?"

"Let me tell you about one of my favorites I met offline."

"Offline?" he was confused.

"Yeah, this one was special, Steve."

"How was he special?"

She smiled.

Ivy Lee

You're Special...

"I'll see you later?" Za-Non asked Sevan, leaning over to kiss her in the passenger seat of his car as he dropped her off at work.

She blushed as she often did whenever he got near her. "Mmmm-hmm," as she leaned in and returned the kiss.

"Have you thought about moving in all the way yet?" he threw in before letting her go.

She sighed and sat back in her seat as she looked down and began to twiddle her fingers as she often did when she was faced with something serious.

"I have...but..."

"But what? You're at my place more than you are at yours...we're already getting married soon."

"I know...and you're right. We are getting married soon so why rush?" she asked, as she looked into his eyes.

Za-Non sat back in his seat and took a deep breath. "I just want you here every day. I want to wake up to you every day.... is that so wrong, Sevan?"

"No. No, it's not, Z. I want that too. But I can't just up and leave Ryan like this. She has to be able to downsize to an apartment she can afford without me when the lease is up."

Za-Non exhaled louder as he looked away and out of the window. She didn't want him to be upset at her, so she tried to calm the situation.

"Hey..." she said softly, as she gently touched his cheek with her left hand and slowly moved him to face her again.

"Let me figure something out, okay?"

She knew she wasn't going to change her mind about leaving Ryan hanging, but she couldn't let Za-Non leave upset.

"Okay," he said reluctantly.

"Let me go into work. I've got a long shift...and you have to go let your parents know that you've found your wife," she said smiling.

"Stop worrying. They'll love you just because I love you," he assured her.

"Why haven't you told them about me yet?"

"I did. I just haven't told them I was marrying you."

She paused. "Well, I told my mother."

"Good. Maybe I'll come back later to have lunch with you both," he said, smiling.

She laughed. "Maybe. If not, I'll just see you at 6:30 when I get off. Let me go before she writes me up for being late," she said, as she grabbed her bag and purse.

He pulled her back and leaned in and gave her the deepest kiss he could give her. "I love you Sevan."

"I know," she said, smiling as she got out of the car and headed for the emergency entrance of the hospital.

Za-Non let the window down and yelled out to her, "One day you'll say it back."

She turned and smiled as she blew him a kiss and turned back around and continued to walk. As she turned around she bumped into an older gentleman. She blinked for a second because the man was the spitting image of her father; he could have been her grandfather or uncle he looked so much like him.

"Excuse me little lady," the older man said as he looked her up and down smiling.

"Excused," she said in a serious but stern voice.

"My, you are mighty pretty," he said, still staring at her like she was a piece of meat.

"I'm late for my shift. Excuse me," she said, as she went to hurry around him.

He laughed as he followed behind her. "Don't let me stop you and the correct response to a compliment is thank you, young lady," he reminded her.

"Oh, yeah?" she said, still trying to get away from him as she hurried to the elevator.

He stood right next to her as they both waited for the doors to open as he chuckled about her feistiness.

"Nurses are supposed to be friendly, Miss."

"Are we? What makes you an expert on my job?" she asked.

He laughed. "I'm a doctor."

She looked to her left as she looked him up and down. "Mmmm. I've never seen you here before."

"I didn't say I was a doctor here..." he chuckled again.

"I don't like games, Doctor," she said, as she hurried inside the elevator not waiting for it to fully open.

He followed behind her and they both stood in the back of the elevator as a mother and her daughter got on and stood in front of them.

Sevan noticed the man looking at the young girl, who couldn't have been more than 13 years of age. He had a sneaky smirk on his face as he looked over her body in a lustful manner.

Sevan knew that look too well. She gripped her bag on her shoulder as she turned her head to give the man her full attention as the elevator doors opened and the mother and child stepped off.

The man never noticed Sevan watching him and had almost forgotten she was even in the elevator with him until the doors closed again.

"Saw something you liked?" she asked forcing him to notice she was there.

He looked back at her with a grin. "I do now."

She knew he was deflecting about him being caught staring at the young girl. Sevan wanted to kill him right then and there.

"What's your name lil' lady?"

Sevan stared at him before answering. He was dressed in a black suit with a white dress shirt with the top button undone. He had a cocky attitude about him and she really wanted to ask him if he was he related to her father because she had never met her grandparents before.

"Just call me Nurse," she said with a side grin.

"Hmmm, Nurse. I like it....no real names. Call me Doc," he said, as he gazed at her with lustful eyes.

"I get off at 3 a.m. tonight," she informed him.

He laughed. "Oh, you don't waste any time. A girl that knows what she wants. I like it."

She studied his eyes and noticed he used the word "girl" when he was clearly speaking to a grown woman. She knew he was evil and she was excited about him.

"No need to waste any time. I think you might be special," she said, as the elevator doors opened to the surgery floor.

"What's your number?" he asked, before she got off.

She paused in between the doors as she looked around and the floor was empty and turned back toward him.

"You don't need it. I'll meet you where we met at 3:15...Doc," she said as she winked and stepped out of the elevator doorway.

He smiled as he adjusted his erection while the doors closed. He was excited about his new fling.

Sevan smiled until the doors completely closed then immediately stopped and her face became cold. She turned and walked away as she headed toward one of the operating rooms. She dropped her bag near the door way as she walked in slowly and saw Ryan preparing the room.

"Hey, girl," Ryan said, smiling as she continued to make sure everything was intact.

"Hey," Sevan said, as she smiled and slowly moved near the table where the operating tools were.

"I feel like I haven't seen you in a long time," she said as she walked over near the sink.

When her back was to Sevan she quickly reached for a scalpel and slid it in her pocket.

"I know. It feels like Z has been taking all of my time."

"Don't I know it," she laughed. "But as long as you're happy, I'm happy."

Sevan came near her by the sink. "Have you seen my mom today?"

"Not yet. I've been so busy today I hadn't noticed if she was even here."

"I can't believe you gave up being a practitioner to be in here." Sevan laughed.

"Yeah, I figure I'll do that when I get a little older. The excitement is in the operating room."

"I guess. All that blood and guts kinda freaks me out. But if you got the stomach for it, Ry, more power to you. I'll stick with writing prescriptions," Sevan said, as she headed out the door.

Ryan laughed. "Yeah, I guess. Hopefully I'll see you later...unless Z's kidnapping you again," she teased.

"Who knows?" Sevan said, shrugging as she walked out of the room and reached for her bag.

Steve decided to interrupt the story.

"You were able to steal a scalpel without Ryan noticing?" Steve asked in disbelief.

"Steal? No... I borrowed it. I returned it when I was done. Plus, Ry is so absent minded that she probably thought she put it up on the table and when she saw it wasn't there just questioned herself and went and got another one."

"You don't think she realized that you probably took it?"

"Why would she think I took it? I don't even like seeing blood and guts and stuff Steve...that's her thing," Sevan said, as

she giggled.

Steve paused as he thought to himself that she was the craziest patient he had ever come across.

"Can I tell you about that evening with Doc?"

"I'm not sure if we have enough time. It's really late." He was hoping to end the session out of fear.

She laughed, "So I met with the Doc during my break and I convinced him to get us a room at a motel," she said smiling.

"What kind of wine is this?" Sevan asked, as she took a large gulp of her first glass.

He smiled as he returned from the bathroom with his shirt off and just his boxers on. He was even built like her father. She began to desire to know if he was her grandfather or uncle maybe because the characteristics were so similar.

"Do you like it, Miss Nurse?" he asked smiling.

She smiled as he got closer to her. "Sure."

"You want to take a shower?" he asked as he poured more wine in her glass.

"I want you to lay on the bed," she instructed.

His face lit up as he immediately dropped his boxers so that she could see his member. He was standing there completely naked as her eyes traveled to his penis. He had a nice sized penis and she could see he was proud of it as if it were his greatest asset. He was in great shape and you wouldn't be able to tell his true age.

He began to move backwards to the bed in the cheesy motel he found on Northfield road. She could tell he came here often. Probably with prostitutes, or even young girls.

As he lay on the bed he began to touch himself to make himself erect.

"I bet you thought that's all I had for you, didn't you?" he said, smiling as she watched his penis grow.

She stood there and took off her scrubs as she stared him in his eyes until she was completely naked. He stopped touching himself as he was completely taking by her beauty.

Her body was perfect, and her confidence was sexy.

"I bet you thought that was all *I* had for you...didn't you?" she said seductively.

"Come here," he instructed.

Sevan took her scrubs and placed them on the chair as she slowly walked over to him and climbed on top of him.

"You are so sexy," he said, as he slowly caressed her breast.

Tonight was different. She didn't look for the moon like she usually does. She didn't feel the sharp pain in her head pop or her soul leave her body. Tonight was special, but she didn't know why, she just knew it was.

Ivy Lee

She began to slowly kiss on his body like Jonathan taught her. He closed his eyes as he began to relax from the wine and her kisses and touches. She had the softest hands and lips.

The lamp began to flicker in the old motel room, giving them a dull lighting. Neither one of them cared; they stayed in the moment.

"Nurse..." he moaned, as his body completely relaxed when she began to lick the head of his penis.

"Does it feel good?" she asked, in a whisper.

"Mmmm-hmmm..." he moaned, with his eyes closed as he slowly massaged his fingers in her scalp through her curly hair.

"Did you think about me all day?" she said between licks.

"Mmmm-hmmm.." he moaned. "Don't stop."

She completely devoured his penis in her mouth and began to give him a full blow job, because in her own dysfunctional way, as much as she hated it, she enjoyed it too.

He began to moan louder and louder. "You sure know what you're doing little lady..."

When he called her a little lady she remembered why she was even there.

"Did you think about that little girl in the elevator all night too?" she asked, as she slowly pulled his penis out of her mouth.

"Mmmm-hmm...wait, what?" he said as he quickly opened

his eyes.

Sevan didn't wait for anything else from him. As soon as he admitted that he was thinking of the little girl she slid the scalpel from behind her right ear, her curly hair allowed it to go unseen, and slid it across is penis.

He didn't feel the initial cut because it was so sharp until blood began to ooze from his penis so quickly. She sat back on her legs with her knees bent as she smiled her sinister smile again.

He looked down to see where the pain surfaced from and as soon as he saw the blood he was about to scream, and she quickly moved closer to him and slit his throat and leaned back to watch him gasp for air.

He didn't know if he wanted to grab his penis or his throat. Her smile was still there as she watched him bleed to his death. His eyes met hers as they begged him for help as tears flowed.

"This is what should be done to all of you child molesters," she said to him before he took his final breath.

She sat there for about five minutes admiring her work, and then she quickly rushed to the shower so that she could sneak back to work before 6:30 a.m., when Za-Non came to pick her up.

Steve was staring at her as his heart broke hearing the story in great detail. She was inhuman in his eyes. Sevan stared back at Steve waiting on him to say something, but he didn't; he couldn't.

"He deserved it, Steve. He liked little girls," she said trying to justify her actions.

Steve stayed silent.

"Any man that can look at a child the way he did is better off dead."

Silence still.

Sevan never took her attention from Steve at all. She just stared at him, wondering what he was thinking.

"Well...say something, Steve."

Steve blinked, and a tear fell down his eyes. "Sevan, that was my father."

Sevan knew it was his father and she smiled. She sat back on the couch folded her arms and shrugged.

"I told you he was special."

At that moment Steve realized her being there was all premeditated. She wasn't there by chance. The entire day was planned out. Steve didn't know what to do or what to say right now. He wasn't sure if she came to kill him too or taunt him about his father.

Sevan slid her hands in her pockets as she sat up on the edge of the couch to see what Steve may do next.

"Why did you tell me all of this?" he asked as a few more tears escaped his eyes.

She shrugged. "I don't know. Confession maybe?" she laughed.

Steve sat up straight and glanced at the door and back to her.

"What are you going to do Steve? Run?"

Steve didn't say a word. He knew Sevan was capable of almost anything and he didn't want to upset her.

The room became completely quiet and it seemed to have gotten smaller to him. He looked at her just before he went to jump up and run, but as soon as he did she quickly moved with him and out of her pocket faster than he can blink came a needle she stabbed him in the neck with and quickly pushed something into his blood stream that made him pause and fall back to his chair.

He could hear everything and see her, but his muscles gave out on him and he couldn't move.

"Relax, Steve, it's just succinylcholine...maybe you know it as Sux....it just paralyzes the nerves and muscles temporarily. It won't kill you," she assured him, as she sat on the table in front of him as she stared in his eyes.

Steve was fighting in his mind to say something, but he couldn't. In his mind he was doing his best to make his body move but it wouldn't.

"I know you think I'm a monster, but your father is the real monster." She tried to convince him as she glanced at her watch.

"Shit, I got about 10 minutes before that wears off." She began to take the tapes that were recorded from their session and throw them in her bag.

"It feels so good to tell someone everything that I told you," she said with a deep exhale, as she rumbled through her bag.

Steve was watching her as he was stuck in a paralytic state as tears slowly ran from the corner of his eyes when he saw her pull out a scalpel and return to sit on the table in front of her.

"I didn't really wanna hurt you Steve. Honest I didn't, but when you got up to run you made me go to plan B. I thought maybe I could confide in you like a normal therapist, but you had to make this personal, all because I killed your molester of a father!" she yelled.

Steve couldn't respond to even try and convince her that he wouldn't tell. He just wanted to go home to his family.

"Ya, know...I'm getting married tomorrow. Can you believe it, Steve?" she laughed, with an excited look on her face.

She looked around the room. *"You think I can take this tape recorder? I need something old... ya know, something old something new something borrowed something blue?"* she laughed.

She glanced at her watch. *"Five minutes left. I wonder Steve, do you still think GOD brought me here? Do you think He will come avenge you Steve or save you? What did you do that I ended up here as your karma, Steve? Got any secrets like your Daddy, Steve?"* she asked as she leaned in to see his pupils closer.

She looked at her watch again. "Two minutes left…… I really want to let you live Steve, but I just can't trust that you will keep this confidential. I'm so sorry."

She stood up and shook her head as she looked down on him.

"This will only hurt a little, Steve. Hopefully GOD will take you before the pain hits." she laughed.

She took her left hand and slid the scalpel across his throat from left to right as the she watched the blood began to pour just like it did with his father. Steve's body didn't even jerk; no movement at all besides his stare with tears and blood.

Sevan waited until there was no more life inside of Steve before she went to clean like she regularly did after a killing and then she went to his secretary's office and removed all files of her or anything about her. She slid everything in her bag and walked to the bathroom to clean her scalpel.

When she was done she stared at herself in the mirror. Kyle and Steve were the only two she felt sorry about killing. She stepped out of the building, being sure that no one saw her as she called Za-Non.

"I was just thinking about you, Beautiful." He said as she could hear the smile on his face.

"Did your parents fly in yet?" she eagerly asked.

"Yep. And they can't wait to meet their new daughter."

"Me too," she said, *as she looked up and noticed the moon.* *"I'll see you in the morning?"*

"I'll beat you there," he said.

"Goodnight, Z."

"I love you, Sevan."

"I know." She said smiling as she disconnected the call.

Something's Odd About Her

Za-Non and Sevan decided to have a small and less traditional wedding. Instead of a wedding dinner they decided to have a wedding breakfast. This would be the time that both of their families met.

Za-Non had only met Sevan's mother, never her father. Sevan never even talked about him and her mood would change every time Za-Non asked any questions, so he just decided to wait until the breakfast to talk with him on his own.

Gianni was excited about her only daughter getting married and hoped that she found someone who would love and protect her. As soon as Sevan shared that she wanted a breakfast instead of a dinner, Gianni decided to have it catered and invited a host of prestige people, just like her 16th birthday party.

Gianni paid for everything; the dress, the catering, the décor, the minister, the food, the DJ...you name it, she paid for it and planned it. Jonathan wanted nothing to do with it, but showed his face anyway.

Sevan was dressed in an ivory sheath column V-neck knee length chiffon cocktail dress with ruffle beading, with a pair of gold open-toe sandal heels by Jimmy Choo. Her hair was done in a neat bun and her make-up was done naturally to enhance her natural beauty. She wore diamond stud earrings and the most beautiful smile. Za-Non was in complete awe at how stunning she looked as he sat with his parents, watching her engage with their guest.

As she walked around to speak to her guests before they ate, she picked up on different whispers of people who assumed she couldn't hear them.

"Cute dress...but who is the guy?"

"I'm not sure, I always thought she was a lesbian."

"I always thought the entire family was strange."

Sevan tried to not let it bother her, but as she overheard more of the snickering and talking she hurried to the bathroom in embarrassment and stared at her reflection in the mirror.

What am I doing? Is it too soon to marry him? I don't even know him or his family. He doesn't even know me either.

Her thoughts were interrupted as the door opened and she broke out of her thoughts and pretended to wash her hands as her father walked in and stood behind her. She was looking down at her hands as she glanced up and the reflection of him caught her off guard. She quickly shut the water off and stared at him in the mirror.

She hadn't see Jonathan in months. He was never home when she stopped by to see her mother and she was perfectly okay with it.

"You look amazing," he said breaking the silence.

"Thank you," she forced out.

"How well do you know this guy?" he asked.

"How well did my mother know you?"

"Sevan, I don't want to fight. I just want to make sure you're doing the right thing." He sounded sincere.

"The right thing? What do you even know about the *right* thing?" she snapped.

"Sevan, do you really think I was bad to you? I clothed you, I fed you, I kept a roof over your head- "

"So, you thought that meant I owed you with my body?" she interrupted.

"Sevan, I did nothing wrong."

She turned to face him for the first time without fear. "You raped me."

"Rape?" he chuckled. "I've never done anything you didn't want me to do."

"What in your sick mind thinks I wanted my own father to have sex with me?" she snapped, as she squinted her eyes at him.

"Sevan, I know you wanted it. Your body told me every time you wanted. You were so desperate to have me that you caused so many problems in my marriage."

Sevan couldn't believe what she was hearing. "I caused problems in your marriage? "she said as she pointed to herself then directly at him

"Sevan, you're grown now. Try and take some responsibility for your own actions." He wouldn't let up on her.

She felt the rage rise in her. "How dare you blame ME for your fucked-up ways! I was a child!"

"Oh, please. You are a female. You tried your best to seduce me until I couldn't take it anymore! Until I finally gave in! You drove your own mother insane to where she had to go to a crazy house for a full month! You did that, so you could have me to yourself, didn't you?"

"Are you fucking kidding me! Is this what you tell yourself so that you can sleep at night? That it was *ME?*"

Jonathan didn't respond. He just smirked. The same smirk she gave Steve her entire therapy session.

"Why are you even here! You're always ruining my important days! Every birthday! My graduation! You cannot have my wedding day! Do you understand me!" she yelled as she moved closer to him pointing her right pointer finger in his face.

"You are so dramatic. I made your life great. I taught you how to be a woman. I taught you how to please a man. Look at you. You graduated college with no kids. You have a career. *I* made you into this woman that he thinks is so wonderful! You are *my* creation Sevan. *MINE!* You should be thanking me."

Sevan paused and became completely silent as she took in

everything he was saying. Nothing she would say could make him see what he had done to her. He was standing in her face putting the full blame on her.

"So now what? Should that be my speech today? Should I tell everyone how grateful I am that my own father taught me how to suck a dick? That I can make a man feel so good with my mouth? That my sex is probably the most mind-blowing sex my husband will ever have thanks to my wonderful father?"

Jonathan's face turned red as he grit his teeth. He had never heard it said aloud what he did and never by her. He honestly believed she would say those things and it would ruin him for life.

Neither one of them said a word as they stared at each other and Gianni appeared from around the corner with tears in her eyes. She had heard the entire conversation. As soon as she saw Jonathan leave the room behind Sevan she followed.

"All this time you tried to make me think I was crazy?" she said, in a low and broken tone trying to hold in her tears.

"Gianni," Jonathan said, as he stepped back in shock.

Sevan leaned against the bathroom sink as she gasped for air. She never expected her mother to find out the truth this way.

"Mom," she whispered.

Gianni stared at Sevan. "I am so, so, sorry," she said still fighting her tears.

"Gianni, I don't know what you think you heard-" Jonathan began his regular manipulation tactic.

Gianni threw her right palm up toward him. "Stop! I heard it all."

She redirected her attention to Sevan. "I will...we will deal with this later. This is your day. I want- I need you to at least have one special day in your life. Please."

Sevan stared her mother in the eyes. She didn't believe she would really deal with it later. She didn't really believe her mother didn't really know. It was the fact that it wasn't private anymore that bothered her. It was the fact it was officially confirmed and right now their picture-perfect family wasn't so perfect anymore.

Gianni walked over to Sevan and fixed her hair and straightened her dress.

"Now, go out there and meet your new family. They're waiting on you."

Gianni had become a master at faking for the public and Sevan didn't even know what was real anymore. She wasn't sure if her mother was serious about dealing with her father or if she would even deal with him. She decided not to think about it and walked out to return to her wedding breakfast.

She paused as she got to the door and straightened up, fixed her face and plastered on the same fake smile that she saw her mother do for guests her entire life. She was happy that it was finally out in the open and a weight was lifted off her shoulders.

When she returned to the table where Za-Non was sitting with his parents he stood up to greet her.

"There you are. I thought you got cold feet and ran off," he said jokingly.

She smiled a half smile. "I would never leave you."

"I sure hope not." He smiled.

"Oh, My Daughter what is the matter?" his mother asked as she reached over and gently touched her hand.

Sevan jumped at the touch and almost rejected her, but then she quickly relaxed.

"I'm ok. Wedding jitters," she lied.

She wasn't afraid to marry Za-Non. She couldn't wait to marry him. She admired him and loved him. She was so lost in the fact her father was there that she hadn't noticed how handsome Za-Non was today. He had on an ivory suit to match her with his top button undone. His hair was to the back like the first day she met him, and he had a slight blonde almost reddish beard. His smile made the entire room warm to her. She felt safe next to him.

For the first time everyone she murdered swarmed her mind. She looked around at all the guest and at each table she thought that she saw one of them sitting with her guest. She blinked a few times and they were still there; just staring at her.

Her palms began to sweat, and she felt herself beginning to

have a slight panic attack. She looked to her left and there was Kyle sitting at the table with Ryan, as she laughed and entertained the other guest.

All she could hear was chatter and laughter as she looked toward the middle table and saw Greg sipping his wine as he toasted toward her and winked. She took a deep gulp and looked to the right of the middle table and Doc was smiling just as he did when he first saw her in the elevator.

She felt like she was going insane as she looked to her far-right table and there was Steve staring at her. He wasn't smiling at all. He was staring at her with pain filled eyes. It was almost like she could feel it and she hadn't felt real pain in years.

"What have I done?" she whispered to herself as she stared back into Steve's eyes.

"What?" Za-Non asked, as he leaned in to her.

Sevan came back to reality as she slid her chair back and quickly jumped up.

"Excuse me," she said, and hurried off back to the bathroom without waiting on a response from Za-Non.

"What on earth?" his mother said, as she held her fork before allowing it to enter her mouth while her eyes watched Sevan hurry away. "Something is odd about that girl," she said, as she finally let the food enter.

Za-Non slid his chair back to go after her. "Nothing is wrong with her. Excuse me."

His parents exchanged looks as their eyebrow raised and continued to eat.

Sevan stood outside the bathroom against the wall and leaned her head on it. She closed her eyes and began to hope she was just hallucinating about seeing all of them. She felt a touch on her right hand and slowly opened her eyes and there was Za-Non.

"Hey," he said softly.

"Hey," she said as she felt herself relax slightly.

"You okay?"

"Yeah. I think I just felt a little overwhelmed."

"Do you still want to marry me?"

"Of course, I do, Z." she assured him, as she looked him in his eyes.

"What's wrong then?"

"I don't know. I had an argument with my father in the bathroom earlier and I just can't seem to shake it." she said being honest for the first time.

"Did something happen?"

"No. He just seems to believe that he was a wonderful father and we disagree."

"He couldn't be that bad...he did raise such a wonderful

woman," he said, smiling as she cut her eyes at him.

"Whoa…. Okay I see he is a sore spot for you. We don't have to talk about him," he said, as he reached and held both her hands.

Sevan gripped his hands for security.

"Can he never be in our lives? Ever?"

"If that's what you want, sure," he promised her. "Only if you promise to meet me at the alter tonight at 7:30," he said, as he put his pinky up to her.

She giggled. "I promise," as she locked her pinky with his.

"Z?"

"Yes?"

"Why was the time 7:30 so important for us to get married?"

"Because that's the time that I first saw your beautiful face," he said, as he touched her cheek softly.

"I love you, Sevan."

"I know," she said, smiling as she reached up to kiss him.

Where did you get this?

The water was so beautiful, that Sevan couldn't stop staring at it. She had only seen blue water in movies, she had no idea that it existed in real life until Za-Non brought her for their honeymoon.

She felt so free right now as she sat on the beach in her royal blue two-piece swimsuit allowing the sun to kiss her body gently while she watched her new husband swim.

She was never into swimming, but she enjoyed looking at the water. She felt like nothing in life mattered but the two of them right now. They were out of the country with no way for others to contact them, except on WIFI.

Her husband had made love to her all morning and all night the first two days there, and for the first time sex felt different to her. She enjoyed it in a deeper way than before. When she would have sex in the past it was always about power with her; with Za-Non it was a connection that she felt in her soul.

He made her body tremble with just the touches of his fingertips and the soft kisses of his lips on her neck. She could still feel him as she watched him swim and reflected on how gentle he was with her.

As he came out of the water and sat next to her she couldn't help but to smile.

"What are you smiling about?" he asked, as he grabbed a

towel and blotted his face.

"Just how lucky I am to have you."

"Is that right?" he said smiling as he tossed the towel at her.

She giggled as she caught it. "Let's stay here forever. Just you and me."

"What about work?" he laughed.

"Let's just pay for a house…cash. Maybe two or three, rent two out and live off of that for forever," she said smiling.

He laughed. "I think the sun is getting to your brain."

"No…and we can make love all day and watch the sun rise and set," she said, as she tried to convince him that it was a great idea.

"What about our family?"

"I can live without them." She smiled.

"I can't." he chuckled.

Her smile disappeared. "But you have me now."

He nodded. "Yes…and I want you to be a part of my family. I can't live without any of you." He tried to explain, when he saw her face.

Sevan didn't respond. She slid her sunglasses down over her eyes and refocused her attention back to the water as the sun began to set.

"Sevan, I don't know what happened in your family or why you don't want to be around them, but my family is really close, and we love each other. I just want you to experience that too, okay?"

She nodded and turned to face him. "Okay."

"Let's go shower and have dinner," he said, as he stood up and reached for her hand.

She paused as she looked up at him and he smiled. She returned his smile as she put her hand in his and stood up.

"I really love you Sevan."

"I know." She said as she tightened the grip as they held hands and walked back to their hotel.

He chuckled. "One day you will say it."

She laughed. "One day.

When they returned to their room, Sevan immediately threw her swim suit off and headed for the shower. She couldn't wait to get the sand off her body.

Za-Non enjoyed watching his wife walk around naked.

"There's sand all in my hair!" she giggled, as she yelled from the bathroom while shaking it out.

"Are you taking a shower with me?" she yelled again.

"Yeah!"

"Can you bring me a razor out of my bag?" she yelled as she turned the shower water on.

Za-Non appeared in the doorway and stared at her like he saw a ghost.

"Z? What's wrong?" she paused near the shower as she stood there naked staring at her husband.

Za-Non didn't speak. He just stared at her. She had never seen him like this.

"Z? You're scaring me...what's the matter?" she asked desperately.

Za-Non held out his right hand and opened his palm. "Where did you get this?" he asked in a low, but nervous tone.

Sevan's eyes traveled to his palm and she saw the rock that she had taken from Kyle after she killed him.

"I got it from a friend," she said nervously.

"You stole it from a friend?" he accused her.

"No," she lied.

"Sevan, don't lie to me." His voice became stern and she instantly was afraid.

"Z, I'm not lying," she tried to convince him, as the steam from the shower took over the bathroom.

Za-Non didn't say anything as he stared at her for a long time. He closed his hand to grip the rock.

"It was you," he said, as he felt a tremble in his voice.

"What was me?"

"They said he came in with a woman."

"Who, Z?" She pretended to not know what he was talking about.

"He didn't have a girlfriend," he said, as he allowed thoughts to escape his mind aloud.

"Z- "

"He never left this rock anywhere."

"Za-Non- "

"Since the day I gave it to him. The police said they didn't find a rock on him when I asked about it," he said, as he squeezed harder.

"It was you," he repeated.

"Za-Non...we need to talk about this. Let's go sit down, okay?" Sevan suggested, in a nervous tone.

"Why him, Sevan?" he said as a tear left his right eye.

"Why who, Z?" She continued to act as if she didn't know what he was talking about.

"Why Kyle, Sevan?" he asked again. "Why my fuckin' brother?" he shouted at her, as saliva flew from his lips.

Za-Non began to have flashbacks of seeing Kyle on the coroners table after coming to ID the body since his mother couldn't bring herself to do it.

"You-" his voice began to crack. "You killed my fuckin' brother!" he said, as he clenched his fist together and put them up to his head as he began to walk in circles and cry with rage and anger.

"You killed my fuckin' brother! Oh, God! Oh God!" he wailed in agony mixed with anger.

His face was blood red and Sevan's heart was pounding as she began to cry slightly.

"Z-" she reached her hands toward him.

"Don't fuckin' touch me! Don't fuckin' touch me!" he screamed in her face.

She backed away out of fear and tears began to pour. "Z, please. It's not what you think," she begged.

Za-Non stopped in his tracks and his tears as he stared at her. "Do you know how much pain you have caused my family?" he asked calmly with a hoarse voice from screaming. "Do you know how much we loved him?" he asked. "He went from foster home to foster home being abused until he came to us!"

Sevan backed into the wall as her tears began to pour. She had never forgiven herself for what she did to Kyle and she had never suspected she was with his brother or that he was adopted.

When Za-Non spoke of Kyle he did it as if he were still alive and he always used a nickname. They didn't even have the same last name.

"Za-Non-" she pushed through tears.

"I fuckin' hate you Sevan."

Sevan felt her entire heart break when he said those words to her. She put her hand across her heart and shook her head.

"No, Za-Non…. please…no…" she said through tears.

The woman he once loved was no longer beautiful to him. Everything about her disgusted him right now.

"I promised him no one would ever hurt him again and the woman I married killed him." he cried.

"Z…please let me explain," she begged.

Za-Non didn't say anything as he turned to walk away she yelled to him, "Za-Non! Please! I love you!" she cried.

Za-Non turned to look at her midway, shook his head as he looked down at the rock in his hand and then back to her.

He had longed to hear those words from her so long, but today it meant nothing to him.

"Good bye Sevan," he said, then turned and walked away as she fell to the floor crying.

Made in USA - Kendallville, IN
1219798_9781978210288